Eye Spy

Garden Girls
Cozy Mystery Series Book 5

Hope Callaghan

http://hopecallaghan.com
Copyright © 2015
All rights reserved.

This book is a work of fiction. Although places mentioned may be real, the characters, names and incidents and all other details are products of the author's imagination and are used fictitiously. Any resemblance to actual events or actual persons, living or dead is purely coincidental.

No part of this publication may be copied, reproduced in any format, by any means, electronic or otherwise, without prior consent from the copyright owner and publisher of this book. The only exception is brief quotations in printed reviews.

****

Visit my website for new releases and special offers: http://hopecallaghan.com

Table of Contents

Chapter 1

Gloria Rutherford couldn't believe the day she was having! She woke up, threw a load of laundry in the washer and then turned it on before heading outdoors with her dog, Mally. When she came back in a short time later, her floor was covered in a half-inch of water. Something she at first, didn't notice.

Mally, of course, went into the kitchen before Gloria. As soon as her paws hit the linoleum, her legs went out from underneath her and she ended up in a wet heap in the middle of the kitchen floor. Gloria tried to rescue her poor mutt as she stepped onto the floor and reached out to upright her. It didn't take long for her to go sailing along the kitchen floor herself. She ended up on the floor, right next to her beloved dog.

Thankfully, neither one of them were hurt. All that was injured was their pride. Gloria could just imagine how ridiculous the two of them looked, sprawled out on the floor, covered in warm, sudsy water.

Gloria had two choices. She could laugh or she could cry. As she looked down at her sopping-wet clothes, she started to giggle, which quickly dissolved into fits of laughter.

Her cat, Puddles, peered around the corner to see what all the commotion was about. He stuck one paw on the wet floor and quickly jerked it back. He licked his wet paw and slunk off. There was no way he was going anywhere near the mess!

Mally pulled herself up onto all fours and proceeded to do the heavy-duty doggy shake to rid herself of some of the sudsy water. She did a pretty good job. Gloria's kitchen cupboards, fridge and stove became coated with the same soapy mess.

Gloria dropped down onto her hands and knees and crawled over to a kitchen chair. She grabbed hold of the chair and then lifted herself up. She was halfway up when she felt her feet start to give out. She dropped back down to her knees and headed to the porch door. "C'mon, Mally."

With one hand on Mally's collar and the other on the doorknob, she was able to pull herself to her feet and wriggle out onto the porch. "You stay out here 'til I get this mess cleaned up," Gloria told her.

She turned to walk back inside the disaster zone when she realized the bottom of her shoes were something akin to ice skates. Ones with nice, sharp blades. So she slid out of her squishy shoes, peeled off her soaked socks and waded through the kitchen to her washer and dryer, which were tucked neatly away inside a large closet on the far wall.

She pushed the knob in to shut the power off. She unplugged both appliances from the wall before gliding across the kitchen floor to the dining room. The water had made it just to the edge of the floor and only the teeniest bit of carpet in the dining room was wet, much to Gloria's relief.

In her bedroom, Gloria peeled off her wet clothes and pulled on an old pair of shorts and t-shirt she wore when she puttered around the house.

Back in the kitchen, she pressed up against the wall, then the counters as she made her way across the kitchen in search of her mop and bucket.

Clean-up was tedious and tiring as she tossed bucket after bucket of sudsy water off the side of her porch and into the grass below.

The task was nearing completion when Gloria's kitchen phone rang. She almost didn't answer it but changed her mind at the last minute. And it's a good thing she did. It was her neighbor, Patti Palmer. Patti and her husband, Jess, had a large farm just down the road.

"Hi, Gloria. I'm sorry to bother you," Patti apologized. "I thought you would want to know that Mally is down here at our place."

Gloria glanced out the window to where she'd tied Mally earlier when she started her kitchen clean-up. Sure enough, there was no sign of her naughty dog.

Patti went on. "Anyways, she's dragging her leash behind her so I figured you didn't know she was loose."

"I had no idea, Patti!" Gloria set the mop aside and reached for her keys. "I'm on my way!"

"That's great," Patti replied. "She's chasing the chickens around the chicken yard right now."

Gloria's face turned red. "Oh my gosh, Patti! I'm so sorry. I'll be right there!" Gloria hung up before Patti had a chance to reply.

Gloria hopped in the car and roared off down the road. Gloria offered up a small prayer of thanks that Mally hadn't been hit! The road was one of the main roads that led into their small town of Belhaven and Gloria knew some of the drivers that flew by were not even close to obeying the speed limit!

Patti was waiting on the porch when Gloria pulled in. Off to the left of the house was the chicken coop, which caught Gloria's attention right away. Mainly because tufts of feathers were swirling around in the air. As soon as she opened the car door, she could hear the chickens squawking and a dog barking.

In the midst of all the chaos was Mally. She was having a grand old time chasing the birds around the pen.

Gloria marched over to the pen, opened the latch and stepped inside. Mally was so caught up in her fun, she didn't see Gloria coming.

Mally raced right by Gloria as she made another dash for one of the terrified birds. Gloria reached out and grabbed hold of Mally's leash. Mally ran until the leash ended. She came to an abrupt stop, then looked behind her.

When Mally saw Gloria standing there with one hand on her hip and the other holding the leash, she dropped her head and slunk over to where Gloria was standing by the gate. She let out a low whine and dropped down on all fours. "You are in big trouble, sister!" Gloria told her.

Much to the chicken's relief, the two of them exited the fenced-in area and walked over to the porch where Patti was watching. Patti covered her mouth with her hand to hide her grin.

"Apologize to Patti right this minute," Gloria told her errant pooch.

Mally dropped down on all fours and buried her head in her paws. She let out a tiny "ruff."

Gloria looked from Mally to her neighbor. "I am so sorry. I hope their feathers didn't get too ruffled out there."

Patti made her way down the steps and walked over to where Mally was still crouched on the ground. "It's okay. I'm glad she didn't get hit by a car!"

She started to pat Mally's head when she realized the dog was covered in a thick coating of dirt. "Wow! I didn't realize the inside of our chicken yard was that dirty!"

Gloria shook her head. "It's not. Mally was wet from earlier."

Patti looked up as Gloria sighed. "It's a long story. My kitchen floor got flooded when my washer sprung a leak. I was finishing the clean-up when you called."

Gloria's eyebrows furrowed as she surveyed her filthy dog. "And now I can add one more thing to my to-do list."

She apologized to Patti one more time before she headed to the back of her car. She pulled an old blanket from the trunk and made her way over to the passenger side of the car. She opened the door and spread the blanket on the seat. Mally settled on the blanket as Gloria slid into the driver's seat. The smell of ripe barnyard manure filled the small space. Gloria rolled down the window and covered her nose with her free hand. "My goodness you smell awful!"

Apparently Mally didn't seem to think so. She thought all was forgiven as she leaned over and swiped the side of Gloria's face with her wet tongue. "Mercy, you stink!"

As soon as they got back to the farm, Gloria tied her dog to the porch railing and headed to the garage to find Mally's bathtub.

She added picking up a heavy-duty leash to her to-do list as she dragged the tub across the lawn and over to the porch.

The morning skies were bright and blue. It was the beginning of a beautiful summer day. A perfect day to give Mally a bath.

As soon as Gloria untied Mally, she sprinted to her tub and jumped inside. Mally loved taking a bath. Gloria made quick work of scrubbing her down and hosing her off.

Mally tried to hop out of the tub as soon as Gloria turned off the hose. Gloria could tell from the look on her face she was headed straight to the garden – and the dirt.

"Whoa!! Oh no you don't!" She led Mally into the house before heading back outdoors. She put Mally's tub back in the garage and hung the hose on the hook attached to the side of the house.

Gloria brushed her hands off and headed up the steps. It was time to look on the bright side of things. Her kitchen floor was sparkling clean and so was Mally.

She grabbed the door knob and started to open the door when she heard the *"toot"* of a car horn. She whirled around and watched as Lucy's bright yellow jeep pulled into the drive, which struck Gloria as a bit odd. Lucy wasn't one to show up unannounced.

Lucy stepped out of the jeep. She shoved her bright red sunglasses on top of her head and wandered over to the porch. Lucy wrinkled her nose as she gazed at her best friend's state of disrepair. "What on earth did you get into?"

Gloria glanced down at her shirt. Clumps of mud from Mally's romp in the chicken coop clung to the front of her shirt.

Gloria leaned over the porch rail and flicked the stinky stuff off. "You wouldn't believe what I've been through this morning!"

Lucy pinched her nose. "Whew! Whatever it was, it smells to high heaven!"

She unplugged her nose and took a step back, out of the smell zone. "Have you been into town yet?"

"Town" was the small town of Belhaven where Gloria lived. Gloria shook her head. "No, but I'm headed that way once I get cleaned up. I need to stop at the hardware store to see if Brian can help me out with my washer. I think the hose broke."

"Something's going on at the post office." Lucy settled back against the side of her jeep. "I can't be 100% positive, but it looks like undercover cops are inside. At least they look like undercover cops."

Lucy went on. "I tried to go in but the door was locked. I caught a glimpse of Ruth behind the counter. She had her back to the door and was talking to some guy I didn't recognize."

"Ruth" was Ruth Carpenter, one of the girls' closest friends and head postmaster at their small post office in Belhaven. She had worked there for as long as Gloria could remember. Ruth loved her job. She was the unofficial gossip of the group and her job was the perfect fit to keep tabs on all the town folk.

Gloria frowned at Lucy. That didn't sound good. Not good at all. "I better get down there and see what's going on," she said.

Lucy climbed back into her jeep. "Keep me posted if you find anything out," she said. She wrinkled her nose again. "I'd change out of those clothes first, if I were you," she advised.

Gloria pulled her shirt forward and surveyed the damage. It was even worse than she thought. "Ugh! I think it's time to throw these things out."

And Gloria did just that. Right after she got out of the shower, she shoved them into a plastic grocery bag and promptly dumped them in the trash can. The one she kept outside.

Mally eyed Gloria from her doggie bed that was tucked back in the corner of the kitchen. "You're on probation," she warned Mally.

Gloria grabbed her keys from the hook, her purse from the kitchen chair and opened the porch door. Mally thumped her tail and let out a low whine. "Not today," she explained. "You're still damp from the bath and I don't want you getting into any more dirt."

Gloria locked the porch door before climbing into her car.

The drive to town didn't take long. Gloria's farm was in the country but still close to everything. Perfect for her to enjoy her small piece of serenity yet still be close to her friends.

Gloria veered into the post office parking lot. She slid the car into an empty spot out front. Lucy was right. There were at least four unmarked police cars parked off to the side. Gloria slid out of Anabelle and made her way to the door.

Through the window, she could see several people milling about inside. One of them was behind the counter, talking to Ruth. Gloria could tell by the look on Ruth's face something was wrong. Her face was pinched and drawn. Her usual happy-go-lucky smile was replaced with a somber frown.

She must've heard Gloria try the knob – which was still locked. She gave Gloria a slight shake of her head before she turned her attention back to the man in front of her.

Gloria left her car in the parking lot and walked across the street to Dot's. Dot Jenkins

15

was another of her close friends. Dot and her husband, Ray, owned Dot's Restaurant, the only sit-down restaurant in Belhaven.

She stepped inside. The restaurant was buzzing. Gloria could almost guarantee everyone inside was wondering what in the world was going on across the street at the post office.

Dot saw Gloria as soon as she stepped through the door. She crooked her finger and motioned her to the back of the restaurant.

Gloria followed Dot into the kitchen, out of earshot of the restaurant patrons. "Something is going on over there at the post office!" she whispered in a loud voice.

Gloria nodded and glanced back over her shoulder, through the large picture window, which had a perfect front and center view of the post office. "I know. I tried to go in but the doors are locked."

Dot peeked around the side of Gloria's head. "Yeah, it's been like that all morning!"

"Poor Ruth. You should've seen the look on her face," Gloria said. Her heart went out to her friend. Something bad had happened and it looked like Ruth was right in the thick of it.

Holly, Dot's part-time employee, popped her head through the pass-thru. "You all talking about what's going on across the street?"

Gloria nodded. Holly came up beside them. "Yeah, that's what everyone else is talking about. Wondering what's going on..."

Gloria glanced at her watch. "I have to run down to the hardware store. My washer flooded the kitchen this morning and I'm going to see if Brian can help."

Brian Sellers was the owner of Nails and Knobs, the town's hardware store. He was a friend of Gloria's. He was also dating Andrea Malone, the young woman that Gloria had taken

17

under her wing after her husband was murdered and Gloria helped track down his killer. "I'll stop back before heading home."

Gloria smiled at a few familiar faces as she made her way out of the restaurant and down the sidewalk to the hardware store.

The bell tinkled as Gloria stepped inside. Brian was focused on something in front of him on the counter. When he finally notice Gloria, a bright smile beamed across his handsome face. "Today's my lucky day. Seeing one of my favorite Belhaven residents first thing in the morning!"

Gloria hopped up on a bar stool in front of the counter and set her purse beside her. "I wish I was here for a friendly visit but I'm not."

Brian leaned forward and propped his elbows on the table. "Let me guess. You've already started on the post office investigation!"

She shook her head. Then it dawned on her. Brian, at one time, had been a circuit court judge. He probably had a pretty good idea who the men inside the post office were.

"Now that you mention it, what do you think's going on inside the post office?"

Brian drummed his fingers on the wooden top and stared at the ceiling tiles. "Well...it's not local or county detectives, I can tell you that much."

He cupped his chin in his hand and glanced over at a customer shopping in the front of the store. The man was digging through a bin of bolts. "I'd have to guess maybe the DEA or FBI," he said in a low voice.

Gloria sucked in a breath and leaned back. "Hmm."

The customer was headed to the counter. Gloria sat quietly on the stool while Brian rang up his purchase.

She waited for the man to leave before asking another question. "What about the FBI?

What kind of stuff do you think they'd be here for?"

"Now that could be just about anything! But for investigating a post office, I'd have to say maybe some kind of theft. Like internet or retail theft," he speculated. "Of course, it could also be drug trafficking. You know, through the mail..."

Brian reached behind him and poured a cup of coffee from the pot. He slid it in Gloria's direction. She lifted the cup and took a sip. It suddenly dawned on her that she hadn't even had a cup of coffee yet, which reminded her of her real reason for being there.

"How handy are you?" she asked.

Brian grinned. "Handy as in 'fix-it' handy?"

Gloria nodded. "Yeah. My washing machine flooded the kitchen floor this morning. That's the real reason I'm here."

"Sounds like a broken line," he guessed. "I can come by after work tonight and take a look at it."

Gloria's shoulders sagged in relief. "I would be forever grateful if you could. I'll pay you," she said.

"No way!" He shook his head and then he had an idea. "How 'bout fixing me one of your famous home-cooked dinners?" He was teasing her. He didn't really mean it.

Gloria slapped an open palm on the counter. "Great idea! You like pasta?"

"One of my favorites," he replied. "But I was just kidding about dinner."

Gloria stuck a hand on her hip. "Well, I'm not! She studied him for a minute. "You look like you could use a home-cooked meal!" she declared.

Brian's face reddened. He really hadn't meant to have her make him dinner. "But what if I can't fix your washer?"

"Then you don't eat," Gloria teased. "I'm kidding! If you can't, that's okay. Six-thirty sound good?" She eased off the barstool and pulled her purse from the countertop.

"Six-thirty," he confirmed. "Oh, and what model is your washer? I'll need to bring some hoses with me."

He jotted down the information before Gloria headed out the door. She'd just seen Paul the night before and she knew she wouldn't see him now for a couple days. She didn't want to bother him with something as minor as her washer.

Maybe she should invite Andrea over for dinner, too...

Gloria wandered over to her car. The post office parking lot was empty now. There was just one unmarked vehicle still parked next to hers. She decided to check the door one more time before heading home.

She walked to the front and twisted the knob. She was surprised that it opened. Ruth was behind the counter. Her eyes were red and her face swollen. Gloria's heart ached for her friend. It was obvious she'd been crying.

Behind Ruth, sitting at a small counter, was a dark-haired man. He had his head down and he was staring at the laptop in front of him. He didn't look up as Gloria approached the counter. "Everything okay?" It was the first thing that popped into Gloria's head. *Of course everything wasn't okay!*

Ruth shook her head and mumbled under her breath. "Can I come by your house later?"

Gloria reached out and squeezed her hand. "Of course. Whenever you want. I'll be home."

Tears welled up in Ruth's eyes. She nodded, not trusting herself to say another word in case she burst into tears again. Gloria gave Ruth a small, reassuring smile and then headed back outside.

Gloria started to climb into Anabelle when she remembered her promise to stop by Dot's before she left. She headed back across the street and inside. The breakfast crowd was gone now. She could see Dot's dark head bobbing up and down in the back in the kitchen.

Dot looked up from the cutting board when Gloria walked through the doorway. "The post office was unlocked. I had a chance to talk to Ruth for just a minute."

Dot wiped her hands on her apron. "And?"

"She's coming by my place later. There was a guy sitting in the back and she couldn't talk."

"Poor thing," Dot clucked. "I hope it's nothing too serious."

"I'll let you know what I find out." Gloria glanced at the clock on the wall. It was just about lunchtime. Her stomach was grumbling. She remembered Mally and Puddles. They were probably ready for some lunch, too. "I better get going."

Back at the farm, Gloria pulled a packet of pasta from the cupboard. She decided to make Brian one of her favorite dishes, spaghetti pie. She peered inside the fridge, checking to make sure she had the right cheeses. She let out a sigh of relief when she saw all the ingredients were on hand.

That reminded Gloria. She needed to call Andrea to see if she wanted to come over for dinner. Gloria reached out to pick up the phone when it started to ring.

She lifted it up and held it against her ear. "Hello?"

At first, all she could hear was the sound of someone blowing their nose, which was followed by loud sniffles. Gloria would recognize those sniffles anywhere. They belonged to Ruth.

"Ruth?"

"Gloria! You're not going to believe this! I've been replaced!" Ruth wailed. "They have someone here to take my place until an investigation has been done and they cleared me of any wrongdoing!"

Ruth didn't give Gloria a chance to answer. "Can I come over to your place?"

Gloria nodded into the phone. "I'm home. You can come by now if you want."

"No. I mean - can I *stay* at your place? This thing has me freaked out! I don't want to be alone and you're the first person I thought of."

Gloria swallowed the lump in her throat. She loved Ruth dearly. But she loved her from a distance. As in, the distance between Ruth's house and her own. Images of Ruth rummaging through her medicine cabinets, through her file cabinets, through her everything - filled Gloria's head.

But how could she tell her friend "no" in her time of need? Gloria took a deep breath and blurted out, "Of course you can!" She squeezed her eyes shut and uttered a quick prayer in her head. *Please, Lord. Help me survive Ruth!*

Chapter 2

The spaghetti pie was bubbling away. The loaf of garlic bread was ready for the oven. Gloria lifted the baking sheet, opened the door and popped the tray inside.

She shut the oven door and glanced out the window. It was 6:25 and Brian Sellers was pulling into Gloria's drive. She watched as he opened the back door of his SUV and reached in to grab a tool box. Gloria prayed he would be able to fix her washer. Now that she had Ruth coming to stay, the last thing she needed was a busted washer. The nearest laundromat was miles away – in Green Springs.

She was going to have her hands full the next few days with Ruth moving into her place until, well...until who knew when.

Andrea texted that she was on her way. Ruth had stopped at her house to pack her bags. The dinner for two had turned into dinner for a few. But Gloria had more than enough to go around. Plus, she just loved the spaghetti pie recipe. It was one of her favorites and one she didn't get to make often since it was only her at the house, and who wanted to cook a big meal for a party of one?

She wiped her hands on her apron before she lifted it over her head and hung it on the hook by the door. She opened the door and stepped out onto the porch at the same time Brian stuck his foot on the sidewalk. "Thank you for coming by, Brian. You have no idea how grateful I am."

He smiled warmly. "Anything for one of my girls," he teased.

She gave him a quick hug and ushered him into the kitchen. She pointed to the washer and watched as he pulled it out of the closet and into the middle of the kitchen floor.

There was a light tap on the door. Gloria spun around to see who it was. Andrea's pretty blonde head was peeking in through the window. Gloria waved her in. She hugged her tight. "You don't have to knock, dear. You know you can just come on in."

Brian looked up from the back of the washer. "Hello beautiful." Andrea blushed and focused her gaze to her ten perfectly-manicured red toes that were peeking out through the cutest pair of wedge sandals Gloria had ever laid eyes on. "Oh my. I love those shoes!"

Andrea twisted her foot for a side view. "Thanks!" Andrea gushed. "I love them. I loved them so much I bought them in every color. Pink, blue, yellow, green…"

Before she could answer, there was another tap on the porch door. This time it was Ruth. The last guest to arrive and the one who looked positively panic-stricken.

Gloria opened the door. Ruth crossed the threshold dragging a suitcase behind her. A very *large* suitcase. Gloria swallowed the lump in her throat. She racked her brain as she tried to remember how long Ruth told her she planned on staying. Judging by the size of the suitcase, it was longer than Gloria had anticipated.

She pushed her fears of invasion aside and hugged her friend in a warm embrace. Ruth released her death grip on the suitcase long enough to hug Gloria back. "Thank you for letting me stay here, Gloria. I can't be alone right now."

Gloria turned to lead Ruth to the back. To the spare bedroom. She caught Andrea's raised eyebrows, as if to say, "Ruth is staying here?"

Gloria gave her a dark look and kept moving. She could've sworn she heard a faint chuckle escape Andrea's lips as she led Ruth out of the kitchen.

Ruth set her suitcase on the bed, unzipped the top and began putting her things away. As in – inside the drawers. Gloria's heart sank. Just a little. It was apparent that Ruth was here for the long haul.

Gloria left her in the room to unpack and headed back to the kitchen. Andrea pulled Gloria to the other side of the room and out of earshot. "She's staying *here*?"

"I didn't know how to tell her no," Gloria confessed.

A muffled voice came from behind the washer. "I think I got it fixed." Brian slid out from behind the machine and pulled himself to his feet. He grabbed the cord that was draped over the knobs on the front of the machine.

He pushed the washer to the edge of the closet and plugged it into the wall. He reset the dial to "wash." It had seemed like eons ago, not just earlier that day, the washer had flooded her floor. Gloria was pretty sure she still had a load of laundry inside.

The sound of the machine filling with water was music to Gloria's ears. Even better than that, once it was full, the floor stayed dry.

Brian placed his tools back inside his toolbox and closed the lid. "Looks like I earned my dinner," he teased.

Gloria reached up and hugged him tight. "You're my hero!"

He grinned sheepishly. "At least someone thinks so." He darted a glance in Andrea's direction.

Andrea stomped over to where the two of them were standing. She crossed her arms. "Brian Sellers, you're just fishing for a compliment."

He raised his hands. "Guilty as charged!" He was still grinning as he and Andrea walked to his SUV to put the tool box away.

Ruth came back into the kitchen. "Can I help with anything?" Gloria's heart went out to her friend. Ruth, the one who was always so full of energy, so full of life, looked beaten down. Defeated.

"Have you eaten anything today?" Gloria asked.

"No." Ruth shook her head. "I'm not even hungry."

Gloria stuck an arm around her shoulders. "Well, you're going to take one bite of my spaghetti pie and your appetite will be back," she promised.

"I know mine is." Brian sniffed the air. "It smells heavenly in here. I'm starving."

Andrea and Brian set the table while Ruth and Gloria pulled the dishes from the oven. Soon, the table was set and the small group was sitting around Gloria's kitchen table.

"Let's pray," Andrea said. She looked across the table at Ruth. "We don't know what's going on yet, but still, the Lord will hear our prayer for Ruth."

Ruth's eyes shined bright with unshed tears. She closed her eyes and bowed her head.

Gloria let Andrea lead them in prayer. "Dear Lord, bless this food we are about to receive. We ask for comfort for Ruth. Lord, we don't know yet what she's going through but we pray you give her peace in her time of need."

Gloria started to raise her head, thinking the prayer was over, but Andrea wasn't done yet.

Andrea continued. "And Lord, we ask that you help Gloria solve this new mystery. Amen."

Gloria added a silent "and quickly" to the end of her prayer.

Gloria passed the dish to Ruth first, who picked the smallest wedge and passed it on to Andrea. Andrea had tasted Gloria's spaghetti pie once before and knew they were all in for a real treat. Her mouth watered as she laid a thick slice of the cheesy pasta on her plate.

Brian passed the plate to Gloria before taking a piece. "Ladies first."

Ruth plucked a slice of garlic bread from the pan and set it next to the pasta. "You've got a keeper, there, Andrea," she told her.

Andrea gave Brian a sly glance out of the corner of her eye. He turned his gaze, his eyebrows raised. "Well, aren't you going to agree?" he demanded.

Andrea took two pieces of garlic bread and set them on the edge of her plate. "Hmm. I'll have to get back to you on that!"

After dinner was over, Gloria cleared the table and pulled out the dessert. Fresh strawberry pie! Ruth lifted a piece onto her dessert plate. "I'm sure you're all wondering what in the world went on at the post office today."

Ruth passed the dish and then speared a strawberry with her fork. "Well, the day began like any other day. Sorting the mail, filling the mail slots. Kenny was in the back sorting out the big boxes, getting ready to load his truck."

Kenny was the mail carrier. He worked in the post office each morning and as soon as the rural mail was sorted, he started his route around the countryside. Rain or Shine. That was Kenny. He prided himself on getting the mail delivered no matter what kind of weather Mother Nature threw his way.

There was also one more person that worked at the post office. Jess and Patti Palmer's son, Seth. Gloria's neighbors down the road – the ones with the chicken coop.

Seth was enrolled in college full-time and worked most afternoons at the post office. He helped load the trucks that came in to pick up packages and bulk mail that were headed to Grand Rapids and the airport.

Ruth slipped a piece of pie into her mouth and chewed. Gloria could see she was trying to gather her thoughts together. "All of a sudden, the front door opened and in swarmed half a dozen strangers. People I'd never seen in the post office before." She set her fork on the edge of the plate and leaned forward. "Except for one person."

Ruth had mentioned a while back to the girls that a stranger had started coming into the post office. A real Nosy Nellie. The woman asked a lot of questions but never shared any information about herself. The only thing Ruth knew about the woman was her first name. "You mean Sharon?" Gloria asked.

Ruth picked up her fork and pointed the tip of the tines at Gloria. "Exactly!" Ruth's eyes narrowed. "You wanna know *why* she never talked about herself? Because she's an undercover cop!"

Andrea sucked in a breath. "She was investigating the post office?"

"And me!" Ruth added.

Gloria had to wonder what on earth the FBI uncovered that would bring them to their little town of Belhaven. She didn't have to wonder long.

Ruth continued. "It seems that there's some sort of fraud," she said.

Brian had already finished his pie. He got up from the table and rinsed his plate. He opened the front of the dishwasher and set the dish on the top rack. "Did they tell you what kind of fraud they were investigating?"

Ruth shook her head. "Nope. Not yet. The detective - the Sharon lady is going to be working in the post office until the investigation is complete. They told me they'd let me know when I could come back to work!"

"You don't think they suspect you, do you?" Gloria asked.

Ruth's eyes teared up. "I asked that same question and all she would say was, *We can't rule anyone out.*" Ruth mimicked the woman's voice.

Gloria had seen her in the post office a couple times. Ruth had her voice down pretty good. She sounded just like her.

Gloria hadn't formed an opinion of the woman one way or the other, but Ruth had. Ruth loved to talk. She loved people and she loved to talk with and about people. And anyone who was secretive or tight-lipped was suspect in her mind. For very good reason in this case.

"I hope they wrap the investigation up quick," Gloria said. Not only for Ruth's sake, but for her own. The fact that Ruth planned to stay with Gloria until she went back to work was cause for a bit of anxiety on Gloria's end.

Gloria was accustomed to having her own space. Her own freedom. She hadn't had anyone living with her for a few years now. Not since her husband, James, had died of a sudden heart attack a few years back.

It was as if Ruth could read her mind. "I appreciate you letting me stay with you until this is over," she said.

Gloria caught Brian's grin out of the corner of her eye. He raised his drink glass to hide the grin but not before Gloria saw it. She made a fist under the table and punched him in the leg which, in turn, made him choke on his drink. He sputtered and pounded his chest.

Gloria raised her eyebrows. "Are you okay, Brian?" she asked innocently.

"Ahem! I'm sure I'll be fine. Just swallowed wrong," he added.

Andrea looked at the kitchen clock above the sink. "I really should get going. I have to be

41

up early tomorrow morning." She plucked her purse from the chair by the door. "Just a few more days and the construction crew will wrap things up at the house, thank goodness."

"I can't wait to see it," Gloria said.

Brian rose to his feet. "I better head out, too." He hugged Gloria when he got to the door. "Dinner was delicious."

She hugged him back. "Thank you for coming by on such short notice. You're a real life-saver."

She watched the two of them leave before she shut the door. Ruth stood at the sink, her back to Gloria. Her hand trembled as she stuck her drink glass in the dishwasher.

Gloria took the plate from her hand. "Here, you can leave that. I'll take care of it later."

Ruth rinsed her hands and dried them on the hand towel hanging on the stove handle. She wandered over to the table and plopped down in the chair. She laid her head in her hands.

Gloria walked over and patted her back. "Don't you worry, Ruth. They'll get this all sorted out and you'll be back to work before you know it," she reassured her.

She didn't wait for her to reply. "I have an idea. Let's take Mally and head out to the porch for some fresh air."

Mally heard her name. She wandered into the kitchen and over to Ruth. Ruth leaned down and patted her head. "I've been thinking about getting a dog. It'd be nice to have some company since I live all alone."

Ruth's little white ranch home was situated on the edge of town, right near the village limits sign. She'd lived there for as long as Gloria could remember.

Ruth had never married, never had any children. A long time ago, she admitted she'd been engaged and the guy jilted her just hours before the wedding. Apparently, it crushed her to the point where she never wanted to try again.

Gloria couldn't imagine not having her children, and even though her husband, James, was gone now, she wouldn't trade the years they shared together for anything. Even the pain and heartache she went through after he died.

But Ruth filled her life with her friends and her work. She never complained about being lonely, although Gloria was certain there were times that she had to be.

The only family that Ruth ever talked about was her niece, Sarah, who lived in Green Springs, the neighboring town.

Gloria knew Sarah quite well. When she was younger, she would stay with Ruth for a week or two in the summer. Ruth would bring her to the post office and put her to work, sorting mail and such. Sarah hadn't been around in a while now. She'd just finished college and had a steady boyfriend. According to Ruth, there was even talk of a wedding in the near future.

Sarah's mother, Lois, which was Ruth's only sister, had moved to Florida a few years back with her new husband. Ruth was the closest thing to family Sarah had left in Michigan.

Mally wandered around the yard as Ruth and Gloria sat in the porch rockers and watched the sun sink down behind the farm field across the street.

Gloria glanced at Ruth. She would be bored out of her mind here at the farm. Gloria had a sudden thought - something to keep Ruth busy while she was here. Something to take her mind off the investigation and the post office.

"Now that summer's here, I've been thinking about having a yard sale," Gloria announced. Gloria had tossed the idea around for a few days now. It was high time she cleaned out the basement and the upstairs bedrooms and got rid of some stuff. She still had toys from not only when her grandsons were little, but toys and clothes from when her own children were young.

James used to tease Gloria that she was a bit of a pack rat. Gloria had to admit it was hard for her to part with certain things. Especially the stuff that held sentimental value. But it was time to sort through it and tidy the place up. She couldn't even remember the last time she'd gone upstairs. It had to be before Christmas!

Ruth stopped rocking. "That's a great idea, Gloria! I have a bunch of stuff I need to get rid of, too."

She tapped her fingers on the arm of the chair. "We could have it on Monday, when the flea market is going on."

Gloria had to agree. That would be the perfect time! The drive into town – and the road to the flea market – went right by Gloria's place. Sometimes in the summer if she had an excess of goodies in her garden, she would haul the old hay wagon to the road and set up a little farmer's market. She would fill baskets full of fruits and vegetables and then sell them.

Every week she did it, she'd sell out and have a tidy stash of cash to boot. Yes, her place would be a great location for a yard sale!

"Maybe we should ask the other girls if they want to clean out their houses and sell some stuff," Ruth suggested. The other girls being the Garden Girls. Their small group of friends. Lucy, Margaret, Dot, along with Gloria and Ruth.

Gloria nodded. That was a great idea! She added that to her to-do list for tomorrow. That way, it would give all the girls some time to get everything together and marked. She pointed to the barn. "We can start storing the sale stuff in there until we're ready."

Mally was back on the porch now. She sprawled out on top of Gloria's feet. Gloria pulled herself from her chair and patted her tired pooch. She lifted her hands above her head in a long stretch. Tomorrow was shaping up to be a very busy day. The first thing on her to-do list was head to the post office and try to find out what in the world was going on.

Chapter 3

Gloria pulled into the post office early the next morning. The first thing she noticed were the two unmarked police cars parked off to the side. They were in the spots that Ruth normally parked her own car. Gloria hoped Ruth hadn't noticed, but she probably had. Ruth had gotten up early and headed out right after breakfast.

She told Gloria she was going to get busy on sorting through her stuff. But Gloria knew what she really planned to do was drive by the post office to see what was going on.

Gloria slid out of the driver's seat and made her way in through the front door. Behind the counter was the woman – Sharon – and a tall, thin man with wire-rimmed glasses. The two of them were back behind the counter talking in low voices.

Gloria dropped her envelopes in the mail slot and then peeked around the side of the mail slots. She spied Kenny Webber near the back. He was sorting through the packages and dropping them into various bins. "Good morning, Kenny," she said.

Kenny whirled around. A smile lit his face when he saw Gloria. "Good morning, Mrs. Rutherford!"

Gloria glanced at the two detectives. They had their backs to Gloria. She nodded her head towards the door and mouthed the words. "Meet me outside."

Kenny nodded. He dropped the package in his hand and headed for the back door. "I'll be right back," he announced.

The woman looked up and nodded. She continued her conversation as Kenny stepped outside.

Gloria met him in the rear, near the dumpster. They stood behind the bushes, out of view of the door. "You have any idea what they're investigating?" There was no need to beat around the bush. Gloria had a reputation around town for her sleuthing.

Kenny grinned. He figured Gloria would be along shortly and he wanted to help Ruth in any way he could. And that meant keeping his ear to the ground. Or in this case, his ear to the back of the post office.

Kenny nodded. "Yeah." He looked around to see if anyone was in earshot. "Narcotics trafficking."

Gloria's eyes widened. "Drug trafficking? Here, in our little town of Belhaven?"

Kenny lowered his voice. "Yeah! From what I overheard, there's some big drug ring in Lakeville and they were using this post office to move the drugs from South Florida to here."

"But why here?"

"Well, if you think about it, Belhaven's smack dab in the middle of the state. What better place to distribute illegal drugs than from here? Plus, this place is – you know – off the radar. Who'd ever suspect little old Belhaven as being a drug haven? Belhaven, drug haven, get it?" He chuckled at his comparison.

Gloria gave him a dark look. This wasn't one bit funny. What would people think if they found out Belhaven was some major distribution center for illegal drugs? Why, their property values would plummet! Who'd want to live here?

Gloria envisioned drug lords roaming the streets in expensive vehicles with tinted windows, walking main street with thick gold chains around their necks and guard dogs...

"Look, I gotta get back to work!" Kenny turned to go. "Stop back later if you want. Maybe I'll have more info." He winked.

"Thanks, Kenny. I'll have to do that."

Gloria wandered to her driver's side door and then stopped. She glanced across the street at Dot's restaurant. Maybe Dot had heard something.

She crossed the street and headed in through the front door. She nodded to a few of the locals as she made her way to the back. Dot was at the sink, rinsing dishes. She wiped her hands when she saw Gloria in the doorway. "I heard Ruth was staying at your place," she said.

Gloria nodded. "Yeah. She's shook up about this whole investigation and didn't want to be alone."

Gloria jerked her head in the direction of the post office. "You hear anything from the diners about what's going on?"

Dot nodded. "They're saying it was some kind of fraud or money laundering or something."

Gloria furrowed her brows. She didn't want to tell Dot what Kenny had told her. At least not yet. She changed the subject. "Ruth and I are going to have a yard sale next week out at the farm. On Monday. We were wondering if you or any of the other girls have stuff you want to get rid of..."

Dot swiped at a stray strand of hair. "Boy, do I ever! I have tons of junk. Funny you should mention that. I was thinking of having a sale myself."

"Just bring it by my place when you get ready. We're going to store it in the barn." Gloria turned to go. "And if you hear anything else about the post office, let me know."

Dot winked. "Gotcha! Say, is Ruth going to stay with you until they let her go back to work?"

"Yeah. I didn't have the heart to tell her no."

Dot wrinkled her forehead. "I'm not sure I could do that. Aren't you afraid she's going to start snooping through your stuff?"

Gloria's shoulders sagged. It wasn't that she had anything to hide or some deep, dark secret she kept from the world. It was more a sense of invasion. Plus, Gloria was used to living alone...

Gloria hopped back in Anabelle and headed home. She breathed a sigh of relief that Ruth hadn't come back yet. Hopefully, the whole yard sale project would keep her busy. Gloria herself could see the days ahead would be dizzying. Between trying to get ready for the yard sale and working on the new mystery, she would have her hands full.

Gloria stepped in to the kitchen and pulled her cell phone from her purse. The battery was low and needed a charge. She plugged it into the wall charger when she noticed she'd missed a call. Her brows drew together.

Paul had called, which was a bit odd. He never called her in the morning. She knew he had worked the night shift the night before. He should be home. In bed. Sleeping. The call came in not long ago. She dialed his number, hoping she wasn't going to wake him up.

Thankfully, he picked up on the first ring. "I thought for a minute you were avoiding me," he teased.

Gloria fiddled with the end of the charger. "Of course not! Something's wrong with my phone! I didn't even hear it ring."

Gloria's hearing wasn't all that it used to be, either. Lately, she had to turn the volume up on the TV to full blast just to hear what was being said.

She hated to admit it, but she was beginning to feel her age. Of course, she still felt good. It was just the little things, like not being able to see to drive at night any more, that seemed more noticeable.

She loved these golden years and the detective work that gave her purpose. The visits to the shut-ins that she and the Garden Girls did every Sunday gave her purpose. On top of that, she had Paul in her life. She smiled into the phone. No. Life was good for Gloria. The Lord had really blessed her.

"....the investigation over at the post office." Gloria had been so distracted with counting her blessings, she missed half of what Paul had just said.

"The Montbay Sheriff's Department isn't helping with the investigation?" Gloria wondered.

"Nope," Paul replied. "Must be something big. What with them bringing in the big guns. The FBI."

Gloria's heart sank. She hoped Paul had a little insider information he could share, but it was apparent he wouldn't be able to help much on this one.

"There's another reason I called," he said. "I have houseguests now. Temporarily, I hope."

"You mean living with you at the farm?" she asked.

Paul sighed. Gloria knew him well enough to know the tone of his voice. It was the sound of aggravation. "It's the kids. Jeff and Tina." Jeff and Tina weren't really "kids." They were grown adults with two daughters who had just finished college. Paul had mentioned a few times that his son and daughter-in-law seemed a bit scatterbrained and were not very good at handling money.

He went on. "They lost their house. The bank auctioned it off. They have 24 hours to move out and nowhere to go so they're moving in with me. Today."

"Did you know they were having, uh-financial difficulties?" Gloria wasn't sure if the question overstepped her boundaries, but Paul was a big part of her life and if it involved him, it involved her - in a roundabout way...

"Hang on a sec," he said. She could hear some shuffling around on the phone, as if he was moving out of earshot. Which was exactly what he was doing. "I'm on the back porch. Tina's upstairs unloading some stuff."

"Sounds like they didn't give you much warning," Gloria replied.

"No warning at all. They just showed up on my doorstep this morning, asking if they could stay here until they saved up enough money to put a deposit down on a rental property."

Gloria didn't say it out loud but she wondered if they hadn't made the mortgage payment on their house, what did they do with the money and why didn't they plan ahead, knowing that eventually they'd have to move out?

But she bit her tongue. It wasn't her place to point fingers. Heaven only knew how many foolish things she and James had done when they were younger. *Older and wiser*, that was the saying...

"I have my own houseguest," she announced.

"Don't tell me it's Jill and her family," he quipped.

Gloria laughed. "Oh, heavens no!" Gloria could just imagine having her daughter, Jill, her son-in-law, Greg, and her two grandsons underfoot full-time. Especially her young grandsons, who seemed to get into a pickle more often than not. No, Gloria would be ready for the funny farm if that happened!

"It's Ruth. She's so rattled about being temporarily out of a job, she's staying with me. She doesn't want to be alone."

Paul knew all about Gloria's close group of friends. Lucy, the wild and crazy one that would try anything once. Margaret, the one who seemed the most judgmental of others but had a heart of gold underneath her tough exterior. Then there was Dot, the mother hen of the group. The one he knew Gloria considered to be the most level-headed. And then here was Ruth. Her dear friend that loved a good gossip and always wanted to be in the middle of all the action.

"So you have a vested interest in getting the post office issue resolved and Ruth back on her normal routine and in her own house," he surmised.

"You could say that. So keep your ears open and let me know if you find anything out," she told him.

After she hung up the phone, she said a quick prayer for Paul. It gave her a bit of comfort knowing that he was going through something similar. It was tricky having people underfoot after being alone all these years.

A car horn honked and brought Gloria from her deep thoughts. She glanced out through the kitchen window. It was Kenny. He pulled up in the mail truck. *Maybe he has new information,* Gloria thought.

She met him on the steps where he handed her a packet of mail. "Here's your mail." He shuffled from foot to foot, as if he wanted to say something but wasn't sure he should.

Gloria decided he needed a gentle nudge. "Did you find anything else out down at the post office?" she asked.

Kenny nodded. "Yep, sure did."

"And?" she wondered.

"Well, another detective came in right after you left this morning. I think he's the head guy. You know, the guy in charge of the investigation."

"Anyways, I figured whatever he had to say was gonna be important so I pretended like I had work to do over by the bins where they were talking."

Gloria nodded. Kenny was turning out to be a good spy, uh – detective, she corrected herself.

"They were discussing something about some guy the DEA. That stands for Drug Enforcement Agency," he explained.

"Right," she agreed. Gloria was old, but she wasn't *that* old. She knew what the DEA stood for. Every good detective knew what that stood for!

Kenny shoved his hands in his uniform pockets and rocked back on his heels. "Anyways, the DEA had this guy under surveillance but nothing concrete. They said he was some kind of king pin and that he ran a drug cartel in our area."

"How does this involve Belhaven's post office?" she wondered.

"That's what I was getting to. The cops pulled the guy over for some minor traffic infraction and when they searched his car, right there in the front seat was a box full of crank! Not just a little, but thousands of dollars' worth."

This one was over Gloria's head. She had to ask. "What's crank?"

Kenny raised his eyebrows. "You know. Methamphetamine!"

Gloria watched almost every episode of *Detective on the Side,* her favorite crime series on TV, and she had never heard the word *crank* used before. She added it to her mental dictionary. "You don't say," she murmured.

"The box the crank was in – it came through Belhaven's post office. That's when the FBI started an undercover investigation of the post office. It's being used to traffic drugs!"

Gloria shook her head. "That can't implicate Ruth! What would that have to do with her?"

Kenny pointed to his chest. "You wanna know what I think? I think the investigators think it's an insider job. Someone inside the post office is involved."

"But Ruth? C'mon, that's stretching it," Gloria argued.

"Well, she is the one with access to everything there at the post office. Unlike me and Seth. We have limited access."

Gloria tapped the side of her cheek. That part was true! She would be the most logical suspect. She opened the post office every day and closed it each night. She was the only one with keys to the entire place. *But Ruth?*

Kenny looked down at his watch. "I gotta go. I haven't even started my route yet. You were my first stop." He jumped through the open door of his truck.

"You've been very helpful, Kenny. You'd make a good detective," she complimented. She needed him to keep his ear to the ground so a little buttering up never hurt to inspire him to help.

He started the engine and shifted the truck into gear. "I miss Ruth," he said. "It's boring without her."

Gloria grinned. "I'll let her know you said that. I'm sure she'll appreciate it."

"Yeah. I heard she was staying out here at the farm 'til this is over," he answered.

Gloria nodded. "Believe me, she'd be much happier back at work."

Kenny pulled out just as Ruth pulled in. Gloria could see her van was filled to the roof with stuff.

She pulled the van over to the barn doors and waited while Gloria shoved the barn door open and stepped to the side.

"You're going to get rid of all of that?" Gloria asked.

Ruth stuck a hand on her hip and nodded at the pile. "Yeah. At first I had just a few things but then I got to thinking and I made this little rule for myself. This is how I decided whether to keep it or to junk it."

Ruth held up an index finger. "One. Have I used this in the last year? Two. Can I still fit into it? If the answer is no, it's got to go!"

Gloria chuckled. "Those are good rules of thumb. I'll have to use that myself," she decided.

The girls made quick work of pulling the boxes from the van and stacking them neatly off to one side.

"I ran into Margaret on my way through town and told her about the yard sale," Ruth said.

"What'd she say?"

"Yeah. She seems real excited. I think she's going to bring some stuff by," Ruth answered.

If anyone had stuff to get rid of, it would be Margaret. Margaret and her husband, Don, had traveled all over the world through the years, visiting some exotic locations, including one Gloria herself had always wanted to visit. Israel. And Jerusalem.

Gloria made a mental note to sift through whatever Margaret decided to get rid of. She had some cool stuff Gloria wouldn't mind having for herself.

Ruth brushed her hands on the front of her pants and waited while Gloria closed the barn doors and snapped the padlock closed.

Ever since the time the bank robber had snuck into Gloria's barn to hide out, she'd added locks to all her barn doors - and she used them!

"I noticed Kenny stopped by with your mail," Ruth said.

Gloria wasn't sure how Ruth would feel about Gloria poking around in the post office investigation. "He said he missed you and that it was boring without you," she answered.

Ruth's face brightened. "He did?"

"Yep."

Then her face fell. "I hope they wrap this thing up soon. I need to get back to work. I have no idea what people who don't work do with all their free time!" she declared.

Ruth clamped her mouth shut when it dawned on Ruth that she was talking about Gloria. But Gloria knew she meant no harm. She just said the first thing that popped into her head. And she was sure others wondered the same thing.

But Gloria stayed busy. So busy, she wondered how she would survive if she did have a 9 to 5 job! Between her gardens, her friends and her investigations, her days filled up fast. Sometimes there didn't even seem like enough hours in the day to get it all done!

"You'd be surprised," Gloria answered. She linked arms with Ruth as they wandered across the yard and back to the house. "One day you'll find out and then you'll be just like me," she promised.

After lunch, Ruth wandered from room-to-room aimlessly. There was no way Gloria could keep her busy at her house. They needed to get out. To go into town and make the rounds. "C'mon, let's head into town."

Ruth frowned. "But aren't people going to start asking questions?" she asked. "What if they start whispering about me behind my back?"

Gloria planted her hands on her hips. "Ruth Carpenter! You know better than to pay any mind to the gossips in this town! We are going into Belhaven and you are going to hold your head up high!"

Ruth stiffened her back at Gloria's pep talk. "You're right! No bunch of busybodies are gonna make me hide out in shame!" she declared.

The girls climbed in Ruth's van. "Let's stop by Andrea's first. I want to see how the place is shaping up," Gloria said.

"Great idea," Ruth agreed.

Andrea's beautiful home - the town's unofficial mansion - was almost finished with its spectacular renovation. Andrea bought the house and immediately began updating both the inside and out. It was fun to watch the transformation. The young woman had done a terrific job of keeping the historical charm, yet adding modern touches and her own personal flair.

There was one other vehicle parked in the driveway. It was parked next to Andrea's expensive sports car. It looked to be some sort of handyman van. Ruth pulled her van behind Andrea's car and the girls climbed out. The front door was wide open.

"Knock, knock." Gloria peeked her head inside the door to announce their arrival.

From the corner of her eye, Gloria caught a glimpse of a black shadow as it darted across the room. *"Woof!"* A sleek, shiny black Labrador retriever pranced over to them, his tail wagging. He sniffed Ruth first, who patted his head. Then he turned to Gloria. Gloria bent down and rubbed his ears. "Well, hello there! Who are you?" she asked the dog.

Andrea barreled through the door that separated the dining room from the butler's pantry as she emerged from the kitchen. "That's

Brutus," she said. "I got him from the animal shelter this morning. The same one you got Mally from."

Gloria was still crouched on her knees. "You did? Well, aren't you a beauty! Wait 'til Mally sees you!"

Gloria looked up at Andrea. "I thought you were going to hold off on getting a dog!" Andrea told Gloria everything. Even though they were just friends, Andrea considered Gloria to be more than that. She was more of a mother-figure to Andrea. One she didn't have nearby since her parents lived hundreds of miles away in New York City. Her parents didn't care for the country and as far as Gloria knew, had yet to come and visit their daughter in Belhaven.

"I was going to wait until the house was all done but I changed my mind," Andrea told them.

Gloria lifted her eyebrows, "Oh? And why was that?" Andrea had enough going on with the major house renovations. She'd told Gloria more than once that as soon as the house was finished, she would adopt a dog, but taking one in now would be too much on her plate...

Andrea rubbed the tip of her toe back and forth along the marble floor, a telltale sign to Gloria there was something Andrea wasn't telling her.

She rose to her feet and took a step closer to her young friend. "What made you change your mind, dear?"

Andrea shrugged her shoulders. Her eyes met Gloria's then quickly looked down.

Gloria pressed the issue. "Did something happen?"

Andrea's shoulders sagged. She knew Gloria well enough to know that she would hound her until a confession was forthcoming. Andrea took a deep breath. "Someone was in the house last night," she confessed.

Ruth gasped. Her hand flew to her throat. "Were you home at the time?"

Andrea nodded sheepishly. "I was upstairs, peeling some old wallpaper from one of the spare bedroom walls. I heard a muffled noise. It sounded like it was coming from the library," she explained.

"Then what happened?" Gloria prompted.

"I ran to my bedroom and grabbed the gun I keep in the nightstand beside the bed."

Andrea had gotten the gun at Gloria's insistence. Ever since a dead body was found in the shed out back, Gloria worried about Andrea's safety and the wisdom of her living in the big, old house by herself. So Andrea and Gloria struck a deal: Gloria wouldn't badger her young friend about living in the house alone if Andrea took a gun safety course and then bought one to keep with her.

Andrea lived up to her end of the bargain. She promptly took the course and bought a gun that was designed specifically for women. After she bought the gun, Andrea set up a small target practice in her backyard. She was even able to talk Gloria into doing a little shooting practice right after she got it.

Gloria herself was surprised at how lightweight the gun was and how easy it was to shoot.

For her Christmas gift, Andrea gave Gloria the exact same one. Gloria kept it in the nightstand beside her bed, too. Except hers wasn't loaded. She was too worried that one of her grandsons would come over and she would forget to put the gun up and that they would find it.

Paul had promised to bring her a special case that was hard to unlock. At least, hard to unlock for young boys, and then she could keep the gun loaded.

"By the time I grabbed the gun and made my way downstairs, whoever had been inside was gone. They were in such a hurry to get out of here, they left the back door wide open."

Brutus flopped down at Andrea's feet. He seemed to be attached to her. "I asked the woman at the shelter to recommend a dog. A good watch dog."

Gloria knew a little bit about dogs. She started her research right after her daughter, Jill, brought Mally to her house and dropped her off. "Yes," she agreed, "Brutus will be a good watch dog. Not so good for a guard dog, though, unless he can lick them to death."

Andrea nodded. "That's what the gun is for. If he can find 'em, I can shoot 'em," she joked half-heartedly.

She motioned for them to follow her into the living room. The living room was one of the rooms Andrea had done the least amount of renovation in. It hadn't needed a lot of work.

The only thing she had done was put a fresh coat of paint on the walls, refinish the beautiful wood floors and polish the fireplace.

They passed through the French doors that connected the living room to the library. Andrea stopped in front of the bookcase. "The previous owners left all these books behind. I started to look through them last night. Some of them are quite old."

Andrea plucked one from the shelf and blew the dust off the top. "Check it out!" She handed the leather bound book to Gloria.

Gloria held the book in her hand. This room was right up Gloria's alley. She loved old books - and libraries! She pulled her reading glasses from her bag and studied the cover. *1877 Book of Poetry*. Gloria opened the cover and fanned the pages. "Wow. I need to come by here one afternoon and sift through this place."

Andrea nodded. "Whenever you want, you know you're more than welcome!" Andrea motioned them to the kitchen.

Gloria slid the book back in the empty slot and followed Andrea.

Ruth brought up the rear as the girls wandered across the small hall and into the kitchen. The kitchen was a mix of sleek modern and vintage charm. Andrea had done a wonderful job of blending the two.

Gloria wandered over to the wall that connected to the hall and the library. "I thought you were going to take this out?"

Andrea nodded. "I am. It's the last project on my list. I saved it for last because I'm still trying to decide what kind of bar area to put in. I'm torn between matching it to the granite countertops or installing something more edgy. You know. Like polished cement or stainless steel."

"What about zinc?" Ruth piped up.

Andrea lifted a brow. "Zinc? I never considered that but it sounds interesting. I'll have to check it out."

The girls and Brutus wandered back to the front door. Gloria could hear a faint *tap tap* coming from somewhere upstairs. She pointed up. "What are they working on?"

Andrea grinned. She shook her head. "Can't tell! It's a surprise."

Andrea walked the girls out to the van. Gloria opened the passenger side door. "The intruder the other night - do you think maybe one of the workers somehow got a copy of your house key?"

Andrea crossed her arms. "Hmm. I hadn't thought about that but, yeah, it's possible."

"Maybe..." Gloria started to say.

Andrea finished her sentence. "I should change the locks." She held up her hand. "Already got that covered. Brian is coming by after work tonight to put a new set of locks on both the front and back door!"

Gloria gave the thumbs up. "I'm glad you told me that. I was going to stop by the hardware store on my way back home and ask him to do just that!"

Andrea and Brutus wandered back inside while Gloria and Ruth backed out of the drive.

The next stop on their list was Dot's place. They pulled into an open spot out front. Ruth slid out of the driver's seat and stared behind her. At the post office. She sniffled and turned to Gloria. Her eyes filled with tears.

"Don't you worry, Ruth. We're going to get this mess sorted out in a jiffy so you can get back to work," she said. *And I can have my place back,* she thought to herself.

The restaurant wasn't terribly busy. Gloria waved to a few of the regulars as she and Ruth wandered to the back. Ruth kept her head down and avoided eye contact with the diners.

There was no one in the kitchen but the back screen door was open. Gloria could hear voices coming from beyond the door.

The women wandered around the side of the butcher block island and out the back door. Dot was at the picnic table sipping a glass of water. Ray was seated across from her, his back to the door. He didn't see Gloria and Ruth come up, but Dot did.

She jumped up from the bench seat and scooted around the side of the wooden table. She wrapped her arms around Ruth and gave her a big hug. Ruth sniffled one more time before she burst into tears. She buried her head in her hands.

Dot patted her shoulder. "I know just what you're going through, Ruth," Dot soothed.

And if anyone did know what Ruth was going through, it was Dot. It wasn't long ago that Dot and her husband, Ray, had a diner keel over right inside the restaurant. The authorities had shut the restaurant down until the investigation was complete and Dot and Ray had been cleared.

"I know, it's just..." Ruth began to wail again. Gloria pulled a pack of tissues from her purse and handed one to Ruth. Dot continued to pat Ruth's back. She stared at Gloria helplessly. "I'm sure Gloria's trying to help, too."

Ruth wiped her eyes, then blew her nose into the tissue. She glanced over at Gloria. "Yeah, she is. It's just hard."

Gloria was quick to change the subject. "How're you doing on going through your things for the yard sale?"

That got Ray's attention. His head whipped around. "Good heavens! The woman has the garage half-full already."

Gloria swallowed hard. With everything Ruth had already brought over and half of Dot's garage filled with stuff, she was going to run out of room in the barn to store it all!

Dot held up a finger. "I'll be right back."

She disappeared inside the kitchen. The girls made small talk with Ray until she returned. Dot wandered back out but stayed by the door, one hand still gripping the handle. "I need to get back to work. I mentioned the yard sale to Margaret and Lucy and they said they had stuff to get rid of, too!"

Ruth and Gloria wandered back through the restaurant and out the front door. With one last look of longing towards the post office, Ruth climbed into the van and closed her eyes. She leaned her head back against the rest. "Please, God. Let them hurry up with the investigation," she murmured.

Ruth lifted her head and put the van in reverse. She started to back into the street. "Can we stop by my place before heading home?" she asked.

Gloria nodded her head. "Sure. No problem."

Ruth headed opposite of the farm as she drove to her place. She pulled into her narrow drive and put the van in park.

"I'll be right back." Ruth was out of the van and had slammed the door shut before Gloria could answer. She shrugged her shoulders. Guess this must be a quick grab something and go.

Ruth was gone only a minute. When she returned, she had a laptop computer tucked under one arm. Ruth set the computer on the back seat, then settled in behind the wheel.

"You could've just used my computer," Gloria told her.

Ruth shook her head. "No. Yours won't work. There's stuff on my laptop that I need."

Gloria lifted her one eyebrow but didn't reply. She couldn't wait to see what kind of "stuff" that Ruth had on her computer that she couldn't live without for a few days.

It wasn't long after they arrived back at the farm that Gloria found out what that "stuff" was. Ruth made a beeline for the kitchen table. She set the laptop on top and lifted the lid. She slid out a chair, plopped down and focused on the screen.

Gloria hung her keys on the hook. She took her sweater off and put it on top of the keys.

Gloria glanced over at the screen that Ruth was studying. It was a bit blurry so Gloria grabbed her glasses from her purse and slipped them on. She leaned over Ruth's shoulder for a closer look.

Her eyes widened when she realized what she was looking at. It was the inside of the post office! "Is that what I think it is?"

Ruth was so absorbed in watching the screen, she didn't notice Gloria was right behind her. She swung her head around. "Yeah. It's the inside of the post office."

Gloria narrowed her eyes. She could see Sharon, the detective, sitting behind the counter. Seth, the part-time college student, was there, too. "Is this live?"

Ruth nodded. "Yeah. A while back, I installed a little camera up in the corner to keep an eye on the place."

Gloria frowned. "Are you sure you're allowed to do that? I mean, isn't that illegal? Government property and all?"

It was Ruth's turn to frown. Apparently, the thought never crossed her mind that it was something she shouldn't do.... "I only did it because I thought someone was trying to break in a couple months back."

Gloria still wasn't convinced. However, it wasn't her place to question.

Ruth tapped the button in the corner and turned up the volume, which didn't seem to help. All that could be heard was shuffling and mumbling voices.

Ruth reached into her purse, which was sitting next to her on the chair. She pulled out a set of ear buds. She popped the buds in her ears and plugged the other end in the side socket.

Gloria left her alone as she and Mally wandered out into the yard. The errands had taken up a good part of the day. Soon, it would be time to think about what to have for dinner.

She grabbed the handrail and made her way down the steps and over to her garden. She picked up the garden hose and turned the water on. It was nice to stand there in the solitude and think of nothing more than making sure her thirsty plants got watered.

Mally was on the other side of the garden, over by the strawberry plants. She watched as the dog tilted her head to the side and nibbled one of the juicy, red treats.

The first time she caught Mally eating a strawberry, Gloria was concerned that they might be poisonous to animals. She did a quick research online and found berries were safe for dogs. Grapes – no. Berries - yes.

Gloria and Mally wandered back inside after the garden was watered. Puddles was curled up on Ruth's lap, napping. Ruth absentmindedly stroked Puddles. Her eyes never left the computer screen.

Gloria plucked one of the earbuds from Ruth's ear and leaned down. "What do you think about pizza for dinner?" Gloria asked.

Ruth didn't bother to look up. She nodded. "Yeah, sounds great."

"Maybe we can order a side of chicken wings or something," Gloria said.

"Sounds great," Ruth replied.

A mischievous smile spread across Gloria's face. "We could finish it off with a pile of cow poop for dessert."

Ruth waved a hand in the air. "Sure. Whatever you want to eat is fine with me." She was still glued to the screen.

Gloria grinned. This was fun! "Then, we can pull the rocket ship from the barn and fly to the moon!"

"This is your place, Gloria. We can do whatever you want," Ruth agreed.

Gloria shook her head and headed to the junk pile in the corner of her counter. The phone book was on top.

Pizza was a treat for Gloria. Something she rarely ordered since she lived alone and a whole pizza was too much, but since Ruth was so agreeable, it sounded perfect to her.

She started to ask Ruth what she wanted on the pizza but changed her mind. Ruth was so engrossed in the computer screen, she was oblivious to her surroundings. Gloria lifted the face of her watch and studied the second hand. It was a full 16 seconds before Ruth even blinked.

The pizza place picked up on the first ring. "Joe's Pizzeria," a male voice said. Gloria was familiar with Joe's Pizzeria. Joe's was a strictly "to-go" pizza place. She didn't order pizza too often, but she knew the owners, Joe and Camilla Guiseppe.

Gloria had met the two of them years ago when James was still alive. They would stop by the farm in search of fresh produce for their pizzas. Green peppers, onions, tomatoes. They came every week like clockwork. Until James died and then they stopped coming.

Gloria wasn't sure if they felt as if they would bother her with the visits or if his death made them uncomfortable and they didn't know what to say. Which was odd since they were at the funeral. Nonetheless, Gloria still liked them and whenever she was in the mood for pizza, it was the first place she called.

"Is this Joe?"

"Yeah, yeah," the voice replied. "Who's this?"

"It's Gloria. Gloria Rutherford."

"Oh. Hey Gloria. How you doin?" Joe's voice traveled through the phone. Warm and friendly. That was Joe. And Camilla.

"Good. I was calling to order a pizza," she replied. She glanced over at Ruth, still engrossed in the screen.

"So you got some company tonight, huh?" Joe asked.

"Yep. Ruth. Ruth from the post office is here. She's staying with me for a few days."

"Oh, yeah. I heard somethin' big was going on down at the post office," he answered. "So are you working the case?"

Gloria grinned. "Just a little. Not too much yet." It was on Gloria's to-do list, though. First thing in the morning. Right after she cleaned out the bedrooms upstairs.

"So what kinda pizza would you like?"

Gloria ordered a large pie with mushroom and ham on one side, pepperoni and extra cheese on the other side. That way, if Ruth didn't like any of the toppings, she could peel the pepperoni off and eat it plain.

"Oh, and a side of medium wings with celery and blue cheese," she decided. Her mouth began to water at the thought of chicken wings. Another treat she rarely indulged in since she was alone...

Maybe this Ruth thing wasn't so bad, after all, she thought.

Before he hung up the phone, Joe told her his new part-time delivery driver, Marty, would be delivering at the house. "He's a good kid," Joe assured her. "He's had some hard knocks, though. Actually, he's my nephew on Camilla's side. He got into a bit of trouble there in the Bronx. You know, the Bronx in New York."

"Oh my," Gloria replied.

"Nah. Nah. It's all good. He's on the right track now that he's livin' with us," Joe told her.

Joe already had a whole brood of his own. "So how many kids you have living in the house, Joe?"

"Ha!" He chuckled. "Too many. I gotta put 'em to work here at the pizza place to earn their keep. Look, I'm gonna get started on your pizza but it was real nice talkin' to you, Gloria."

Gloria hung up the phone and smiled. Joe and Camilla were good people. The nephew was in good hands with them. If anyone could straighten the youngster up, it would be Joe and Camilla.

Gloria left Ruth at the table and headed into the living room. She grabbed the remote and plopped down in her recliner. Puddles wandered in from the kitchen and prowled across the room to Gloria's chair. The cat hesitated for a fraction of a second before leaping into the chair and Gloria's lap. He nudged his head on her arm, demanding to be petted that instant. "Well, look at who we have here? Did you give up on Ruth?" Gloria scratched underneath his chin.

The cat purred loudly, circled Gloria's lap a few times and then settled in. Mally eyed Puddles, who looked quite comfy on Gloria's lap. She wasn't about to have any of that! She sat down at the end of the recliner and began to whine.

"Okay, you too." Gloria flipped the lever on the side to lift the footrest – Mally's signal to climb aboard. The three of them stayed there until the doorbell chimed, just as the evening news ended. Gloria started to get up, but then paused. She wondered if Ruth would answer.

When the doorbell chimed a second time, she knew the answer was "no." Then she remembered the earplugs. She nudged Mally from the footrest and set Puddles on the floor.

She could see a young face at the kitchen door, peering in. Ruth still didn't budge. Even when Gloria opened the door, set the pizza on the table and handed the young man a $20 bill. "You can keep the change," she told him.

"Thanks." He grinned and revealed a dimpled chin. "I better get going. I got a few more pies to drop off." He didn't wait for a reply as he bounded down the steps and back to the beat up pick-up truck that he had left running.

Gloria glanced at the computer screen as she passed by the table on her way to the cupboard to grab a couple paper plates. The inside of the post office was empty. She looked at the clock. That's because it was closed!

She pulled the ear bud from Ruth's ear. "Pizza's here."

Ruth jumped. "Oh, yeah." She noticed the pizza box on the table. "Wow, I didn't even know it was here."

She pulled the buds from her ear and closed the lid on the computer. She set both in the chair beside her.

Gloria reached into the fridge and grabbed a Diet Coke. "Want one?"

Ruth nodded. "Sure. I love Diet Coke."

Gloria grabbed a second one, set the sodas on the table and pulled out a chair. She opened the lid on the pizza box and handed a plate to Ruth.

"What kind is this?" Ruth didn't wait for a reply. She grabbed a slice of pepperoni with extra cheese and three chicken wings. She took a bite of pizza and turned to Gloria. "How did you know pepperoni pizza was my favorite?"

Gloria grinned. She grabbed a slice of ham and mushroom. "Just a wild guess." She popped a mushroom in her mouth and nodded at the closed computer. "The post office was closed and you were still watching it..."

Ruth nibbled on the edge of a wing. "Mmm...spicy even." She peeled a piece of meat off and popped it in her mouth. "I was just about to close the cover on it, right after that Sharon lady locked the front door, but something told me not to. So I waited."

Gloria leaned forward. This was right up her alley! "And?"

"I heard a noise. You know, like a doorknob rattling."

"Did someone go inside?" Gloria bit into her pizza.

Ruth nodded. "I could hear footsteps but the dang camera is turned the wrong way. Whoever it was - was out of view. Like they somehow knew about the camera."

Ruth went on. "Then I could hear thumps. Not like pounding thumps but more of a..."

Ruth's eyes shot up. She stared at the ceiling. "The kind of noise you would hear if boxes were being tossed around."

Gloria set her half-eaten piece of pizza on the plate. "Why didn't you come get me?" she demanded. "We could've jumped in the car and gone down there. Maybe even caught the criminal red-handed."

Ruth's face grew grim. She leaned forward. "I started to get up to do just that and then I heard the door slam and it was silent."

She shook her head and grabbed another wing. "Something or someone spooked them and they left in a big hurry!"

Gloria took a big swig of Diet Coke and slammed the can down on the table. "Sounds like it's time for a stakeout!" she announced.

Chapter 4

Gloria spent the next morning sorting through boxes of trinkets and bags of clothes in the bedrooms. There was so much to get rid of, it was a bit overwhelming. She spent a good part of her morning filling bag after bag.

In the back of her mind, she knew she would have to sort through all the stuff and tag it. When she got to the tenth trash bag, it was time to stop. One more bag and she'd be trapped upstairs. The doorway at the bottom of the stairs was partially blocked from all the bags she'd thrown down.

She made her way to the bottom of the stairs, shoved the bags aside and stepped into her dining room. Ruth was waiting for her at the bottom, her hands on her hips. "And I thought I had a lot of stuff."

"Well, I had three kids," Gloria argued.

"True," Ruth admitted. She reached down and grabbed two bags before heading to the back door. "You know you have to mark all this stuff," she pointed out.

Gloria trailed behind her, dragging two bags as she went. "I have a plan."

Ruth stopped to open the kitchen door. "Oh? And what's that?"

The two started across the drive. "You know how some stores have bins? The ones that say $2.99 or $3.99 or whatever?"

"Yeah?" Ruth waited while Gloria unlocked the barn door and shoved the heavy door to the side. "Well, what if I did that? Have a bunch of bins with a bunch of different prices?"

Ruth snapped her fingers. "That's a brilliant idea – but say we *all* wanted to do that?"

"We could put little dots on the items. Pink for the stuff that's $2.99, green for the $1.99 stuff and so on. If we stick together during the sale, we can all decide whose stuff is what. We just have separate sheets of paper and when an item is sold, we take the sticker off and put it on the person's sheet."

Ruth dropped the bag in what was unofficially Gloria's section. "Sounds like a plan!"

They moved the rest of the bags into the barn and Gloria decided it was time to stop for the day. Ruth stepped into the kitchen and plopped down in front of the computer.

Gloria followed her in and headed to the kitchen sink. She washed her hands and nodded to the laptop. "Anything new?

"No!"

She pulled the leftover pizza from the night before from the fridge and popped it into the microwave. "Still want to do the stakeout tonight?"

That question seemed to cheer Ruth. She perked right up. "Of course. I already have my outfit picked out!"

The girls munched on the pizza and discussed strategies. In the past, Gloria almost always did a stakeout alone. This time she would have company. She didn't see Ruth being much of a problem... at least she hoped not.

Gloria's eyes slid over to Ruth, who was sitting beside her in the passenger seat. The car was tucked away, out of sight, in the alley behind the post office. They were parked at just the right angle to have an unobstructed view of the back of the post office – and the rear entrance.

Gloria smiled every time she looked at Ruth's outfit. Her friend was shrouded in black.

Black pants, black t-shirt, black socks! She even had on a black ball cap.

The sun had set hours ago. Gloria reached over and plucked Ruth's black sunglasses from her face. "You don't need those anymore," she pointed out.

Ruth shoved the sunglasses inside her purse. "I almost forgot I still had them on." Her eyes never wavered, never left the back door of the post office.

Gloria had to admit, the woman was tenacious. She made a mental note to remember that if she needed an eagle-eye with her on a stakeout, Ruth would be the one to ask.

Gloria looked up at the sky. Soon it would be pitch-black out. A small mercury lamp hung low over the back door, which gave off some light, but unless they watched the door every second, it would be easy to miss someone sneaking inside.

Gloria checked her cell phone lying in her lap. She was waiting for Paul to call. She had left a message for him earlier. She hadn't heard from him in a few days now. Not since his children had moved in. The poor man had his hands full.

Gloria looked at Ruth in the passenger seat. She had her hands full, too. They needed to turn this investigation up a notch or Ruth would be living with her until Christmas!

Ruth reached over and whacked Gloria's arm. "Hey! I just saw something!"

Gloria followed her gaze. There was a small movement, over in the bushes on the other side of the building.

Ruth reached into her bag and pulled out a set of binoculars. She lifted them to her face and adjusted the dial with her index finger. "You see that? Someone's out there!"

Gloria squinted and stared. "Nope!" She was a bit disappointed in herself for not remembering her own binoculars. That was Detective Work 101. Don't forget the binoculars! She chalked it up to being distracted over the new houseguest and having to clean the upstairs bedrooms.

She wondered what on earth she was thinking when she suggested a yard sale. The crazy thing had ballooned and taken on a life of its own. As of today, Gloria's barn was half-full. Lucy had stopped by with a bunch of stuff, then Margaret had popped in. The entire back of her SUV crammed full. And Dot? Dot stopped by with a loaded van, then came back with another second load!

Ruth reached for the door handle. Gloria could tell from the look on her face that she planned on confronting the intruder!

Gloria grabbed her arm. She'd been through enough of these investigations to know that was a mistake! "You can't do that!"

"But someone just slipped behind the bushes!" Ruth pivoted in the passenger seat. "This could be our guy!"

"And what if "our guy" has a gun?"

"Oh." Ruth's face was crestfallen. She let go of the door handle.

"We watch and wait," Gloria told her.

Patience wasn't one of Ruth's stronger suits. Not that it was Gloria's, either.

Ruth crossed her arms and pouted. "I wish I had my computer so I could see if they went inside."

Gloria caught a movement. The lid of the dumpster flew straight up in the air and then dropped back down. "No. They're not inside. Whoever it is - is in the dumpster."

Ruth jerked the binoculars back to her face. "Yeah, I see. What on earth???"

Without warning, the lid slammed shut and the dark figure darted around the side of the post office.

Ruth pointed. "We need to follow them!"

Gloria threw the car in drive, stomped on the gas and swerved to the left. Gravel flew in the air as she spun out of the spot. She made a sharp right in front of the building, then she stopped. Her heart sank. "You see anything?"

Ruth rolled down the car window and stuck her head out. Her face fell. "No. I think they're gone!" She slapped the palm of her hand on the top of her leg. "I knew I should've gone after them!"

Gloria shook her head. She made a mental note to keep a closer eye on Ruth. The woman was going to get hurt if she kept that up.

Ruth was still in bed the next morning when Gloria snuck out. Well, not really snuck out. She just didn't tell Ruth she was leaving.

Gloria had wandered out to the kitchen in the middle of the night for a drink of water and found Ruth still glued to the computer monitor.

Gloria grabbed her purse from the chair and her car keys from the hook by the door. The first stop on her list was to run by the post office to see if Kenny had been able to find anything else out. She wanted to catch him before he started his route.

Gloria wandered into the post office and headed to the counter. Kenny wasn't in back sorting boxes. She leaned over the counter and glanced behind the mail slots.

"Can I help you?" Sharon, aka the detective, was at the counter now.

"Yeah. I'm looking for Kenny."

Sharon narrowed her eyes. She peered down the front of her nose as she studied Gloria. "He's not here."

"Oh, I'll just come back later," Gloria replied. "When do you think he'll be back?"

"When our investigation is over," Sharon answered.

Gloria's eyes widened. Did that mean they considered Kenny to be a suspect now, too?

Gloria opened her mouth to speak and then clamped it shut. She dropped her mail in the slot and exited the post office without saying another word. Gloria slid into her car and headed out of town. To Kenny's place.

Kenny had lived in the same house for years. It was a cute little bungalow. One that looked like it belonged on the beach. The wood exterior was painted the palest shade of blue. The windows were trimmed in white, which was a perfect match for the small white porch that covered the front.

Tara, Kenny's ex-wife, and he had divorced a few years back. Tara had worked at Prestige Motors, the largest car dealership in the county. It was in Green Springs. She'd worked her way up from part-time receptionist to office manager and was eventually promoted to manager of the finance department. She and Kenny had lived the American Dream. Both had good jobs making decent money. They had spent their time traveling around the world and buying an array of toys. ATV's, snowmobiles, boats....

Yeah, things had been going good for the two of them. Then, one day out of the blue, Tara walked out on Kenny. Rumor had it that Tara had run off with her boss. Not that Kenny ever shared with Gloria what exactly had happened. But Ruth knew. Ruth had taken Kenny under her wing and Gloria knew he felt an unwavering sense of loyalty to Ruth, who was also his boss.

Gloria pulled in the paved drive and climbed out of the car. She made her way down the small sidewalk and up the three steps to the front door. She lifted her hand and started to knock when the door flew open. Gloria's mouth opened at the same time the door opened.

Even though there was a screen separating them, she got a good look at Kenny's disheveled state. A day old beard framed his face and dark stubble covered his upper lip. Part of his hair was matted to the side of his head while other parts stuck straight up in the air. This was not the neatly-groomed Kenny that Gloria knew.

He pushed the screen door open. "You can come in." He stepped aside and watched as Gloria made her way past him and into the cozy living room. She exhaled the breath she'd been holding. At least his house was still in order.

Gloria stepped over to the antique rocker in the corner. The one that faced the floral sofa. Tara had done a beautiful job decorating the place. It was a shame she wasn't around to enjoy it. But that was her loss.

Kenny plopped down on the sofa. He cupped his head in his hands and looked at Gloria with drooping eyelids. "You heard, huh."

Gloria nodded. "I just stopped by the post office and found out you were let go until the investigation is complete."

"Just like Ruth," he said. "Remember when I told you I thought the DEA thought it was an inside job?"

He went on. "So I guess they suspect Ruth or me?"

Gloria nodded. "But what about Seth?" Seth was the college kid that worked a few days a week sorting boxes and packages to load on the trucks.

Kenny shrugged. "He doesn't have access to stuff. You know, like Ruth and I have."

True, but Gloria couldn't rule him out. Gloria remembered the mysterious dumpster diver from the night before. The one that she and Ruth had spotted during the stakeout. Maybe it wasn't an inside job. Maybe it was an *outside* job.

"Before I got the boot yesterday, I overheard the two agents. They said they had who they thought was the ringleader of the group in custody, but he wasn't talking."

Gloria tapped the side of her cheek. "Then they're after the middle man. The one in between that has some connection to the post office."

"They brought Tammy Dillon over to fill in since Ruth and I are gone."

Tammy Dillon ran the post office over in nearby Fenway. It was a lot smaller than the one in Belhaven. At one time, the building had been a gas station before it was converted into the post office.

Gloria wondered what Ruth would think about Tammy being her temporary replacement. Ruth had told Gloria a while back that she heard Tammy was being considered for Belhaven's postmaster position when Ruth eventually retired.

Kenny stood up. "You want some coffee or something?" he asked.

Gloria shook her head. She stared out the window and waited for Kenny to return. She glanced in the direction of the kitchen. Of course, Kenny was still a suspect.

It wouldn't hurt for Gloria to get a peek inside his house. She jumped out of her seat and followed him into the kitchen. "I'm sorry, Kenny. I changed my mind. I'll take that cup of coffee if you have any left."

Kenny nodded and grabbed a cup from the cupboard. Gloria wandered over to the kitchen sink. She looked to the left, past the kitchen and down the hall. It was empty. Her gaze drifted to the backyard.

There was a large storage shed in the corner, right next to a garden. "Your garden looks like it's shaping up," she said.

"Thanks." Kenny handed her the mug of steaming coffee. Her eyes wandered to the right. One of the shed doors was open and she could see inside. There was stack after stack of white boxes. Post office boxes. They lined both sides of the shed. A narrow aisle ran through the center.

Kenny set his coffee cup down. "Now I know I shut the shed door!" Kenny darted down the back steps and over to the shed. He slammed the door shut and flipped the latch in place. He snapped the padlock in place.

Gloria watched as he headed back up the steps. "I hope no one's been messing around out there," he said.

Kenny grabbed his coffee and a box of donuts off the top of the fridge and headed back to the living room. Gloria trailed after him.

She studied Kenny as he reached inside the box of donuts. "Want one?" He handed her a napkin and passed the box to her. She plucked out a chocolate covered donut and nibbled the edge.

"Maybe there doesn't have to be a middle man. You know. Maybe you just innocently delivered narcotics to a drug dealer..."

Kenny reached for a second donut. "That's what I thought," he said.

Gloria polished off the last of her donut and drained the last drop of coffee from her cup. "I better get going. I have some more stops to make."

She added Seth Palmer to her list of people to talk to. The investigators at the post office might be a little loose at the lips when Seth was around, thinking of him as just a kid. Seth was young, but he was smart as a whip. Gloria knew better than to just write him off.

Gloria headed back into town. Andrea's sports car was parked in front of the hardware store. She pulled into the empty spot beside her and headed inside. Maybe one of them had heard chitchat about the case.

Gloria opened the door and stepped inside. She heard the tinkle of laughter coming from the back. Brian leaned over and caught a glimpse of Gloria. "Uh-oh, we've been busted," he teased.

Andrea giggled. Her head popped into view. A smile warmed her pretty face. They both turned and faced Gloria. "How's the washer holding up?"

Gloria hopped up on the barstool and plunked her purse down beside her. "Just dandy, thanks to you!"

"You get the locks changed on Andrea's place?" she asked.

The smile left Brian's face. "Yes, ma'am. Did that the other day. Right after Andrea told me what happened."

Andrea wandered around the side of the counter and jumped up on the chair beside her friend. "I heard you were having a yard sale."

Gloria must've gotten that "deer in the headlight" look on her face. Andrea touched her arm. "No, no. I'm not bringing anything over. Dot told me your barn is already quite full!"

Gloria sighed. "Yeah, this thing has taken on a life of its own. You wouldn't believe all the stuff…"

"Cool stuff, I'm sure. I want to be one of your best customers," Andrea said. "I still have lots of spots to fill in my place."

The previous owners had left all the furnishings in Andrea's house, with the exception of a few personal items. Andrea had kept some of the furniture that was in good shape, and what she had kept fit the décor to a "t" but there were spots that still needed to be filled.

"The plan is for next Monday. We'll open early. You can come by the night before or first thing in the morning to shop if you want," Gloria replied.

Brian held up the pot of coffee and cup. "Want some?"

She shook her head. "No. I just had some over at Kenny's place."

Brian poured two cups. He slid one towards Andrea and cradled his own. "So you must be here to see if we heard anything."

Brian lowered his voice, although there was no one was in the store to eavesdrop. "I'm keeping my ear to the ground for you," he assured her. "The detectives suspect an inside job," he added.

Gloria was frustrated. "That's what I heard – but why? Why does it have to be an inside job?"

Brian drummed his fingers on the counter and stared up at the tin ceiling panels. His eyes met Gloria's and he shrugged. "Well, it's possible someone tipped them off. Or another possibility is that, depending on how long the investigation was going on before they tipped their hand, they may already have a suspect in mind."

Gloria remembered Kenny's shed. How it was crammed full of post office boxes. *Was he running an illegal drug ring from his place?* she wondered.

She thought about Ruth's spy cam she had installed in the post office. "Say, hypothetically speaking, someone installed a surveillance camera inside a government building. Like a bank or a post office, for example, and they didn't have," Gloria raised her hands and made the quote signals with her fingers, "'permission' to do it, is that a federal offense?"

Brian leaned forward, his brilliant blue eyes honed in on Gloria. "I would have to tell you not to do that. You could get in big trouble," he warned.

Gloria swallowed hard. That was the sternest reprimand Brian had ever given her. She didn't take the warning lightly. She stood straight up. "I would never do such a thing," she replied. No, she wouldn't, but Ruth had!

Andrea swiveled around in the chair. "Why don't you do your own stakeout?" she asked.

Gloria smiled sheepishly.

Andrea nodded. "Ohhh...so you already have...."

"Ruth and I caught someone sneaking around the dumpster out behind the post office last night. Dumpster diving. Isn't that what they call it?"

"Then what happened?" Brian wondered.

"They disappeared without a trace," she admitted. Gloria glanced at her watch. "I better go. I need to stop by Dot's before I head home," she said.

Gloria stepped out of the hardware store and headed down the sidewalk. The weather was nice so she decided to stretch her legs and walk to Dot's Restaurant.

The phone in her pocket vibrated. She veered off to the side and perched under the drugstore awning. She pulled her glasses from her purse and glanced down at her phone. There was a message from Paul.

"Sending out an SOS! I need to escape my own house!" The frantic text continued. "Can I take you to dinner?" Gloria grinned. Paul was in the midst of his own crisis and unexpected houseguests. She missed him, but what with Ruth underfoot, a yard sale in full swing and a mystery to solve, Gloria didn't know if she was coming or going anymore.

Yes, an evening with Paul was just what she needed. "That would be wonderful," she texted back. She couldn't wait to see what he came up with. Guests in his house, guests in her house. They'd have to plan a rendezvous!

Dot's place was packed with the lunch crowd. Dot nodded to her a couple times as she hustled back and forth between the kitchen and the dining room. Holly, Dot's part-time waitress, was there, too. She was running back and forth like a chicken with her head cut off.

Gloria rolled up her sleeves and headed to the pass-thru window. "How can I help?"

Dot looked up from the fryer. She swiped a long strand of hair out of her eyes and tucked it behind her ear. "If you don't mind, can you make the rounds with coffee and ice water?"

Dot didn't wait for an answer. Instead, she grabbed the pot from the burner, shoved the full coffee carafe in Gloria's hand and disappeared. Gloria set the coffee pot down, grabbed a spare apron off the hook by the door and slipped it over her head. She picked the pot back up and headed to the front.

She wandered from table-to-table refilling coffee cups and picking up empty plates. Carl Arnett and Al Dickerson were in the corner. They both had empty coffee cups. Gloria headed to their table. She refilled their cups and Al looked up. "Dot put you to work, huh?"

"I offered," Gloria answered.

Carl spoke up. "Heard Ruth's staying out at your place," he said.

Gloria nodded. "For a few days."

Al leaned back in his chair as Gloria grabbed his empty soup bowl. "That's a shame 'bout Kenny," he said.

126

Gloria raised her eyebrows. She didn't want to let on she knew anything about Kenny. Maybe Al heard something Gloria hadn't.

Al went on. "Yeah, my cousin, he works in some kind of intelligence agency there in Lansing." Al lowered his voice. "He heard they were bringing down a big drug cartel here in this area and they were about to take down the ringleader."

Al had Gloria's undivided attention. She heard they already had the drug ringleader and were looking for the middle-man now. She didn't mention that to Al or Carl. Instead, she said, "You don't say..."

Carl wiped the edges of his mouth and threw the napkin on top of his empty plate. "They need to get the riff-raff off our streets. Can you imagine what this is doing to our property values?"

Gloria had the exact same thought. She nodded. "I know! I better get back to work," she said.

By the time she refilled all the coffee cups and water glasses, the place started to empty out. She wandered back into the kitchen where Dot was stacking plastic containers full of pickles and tomatoes inside the refrigerator. She spied Gloria carrying an empty coffee pot. "Thanks for helping out!"

Gloria untied the aprons strings and lifted the apron over her head. She hung it back on the hook where she'd found it. "You know I don't mind." She eyed Dot. "I have to say, though, doing it every day - day in and day out, would wear on me after a while."

Dot shrugged. "You get used to it." She changed the subject. "How are you and Ruth surviving each other?"

Gloria picked up her purse and fiddled with the clasp. "Not bad. She's no problem. But she's chomping at the bit to get back to work." That was an understatement.

Dot shut the refrigerator door. "Maybe we need a Garden Girls meeting. We can put our heads together like we did when someone got poisoned here at the restaurant."

Gloria nodded. It was true. The girls were great at helping Gloria solve her mysteries.

Back at the farm, Gloria found Ruth in the kitchen. At the table. Glued to the monitor. She didn't look up as Gloria let herself in. She probably hadn't even heard her. An earbud was firmly planted in each ear. But she did notice Gloria.

"They think its Kenny," Ruth whispered.

Gloria's stomach grumbled. She hadn't eaten yet, except for the donut. She pulled roasted turkey, sliced cheddar cheese and a jar of mayo from the fridge and spread them out on the table. Next, she pulled a loaf of bread from the bread box and a knife from the silverware drawer. "Are you hungry?"

Ruth shook her head. "No. I ate a little while ago." She pointed at the turkey. "That's some good stuff." Gloria looked down. It was good stuff. Her favorite and one of her splurges at the grocery store. She pulled two slices of bread from the wrapper and laid them on a clean paper towel. She spread a thick layer of mayo on each side of the bread and then placed a slice of cheese on top.

Puddles and Mally knew it was lunch time. They wandered into the kitchen and plopped down at her feet. Two furry faces stared straight at her. Without blinking. She sighed and grabbed a slice of meat for each. They sure did have her trained!

With her sandwich assembled and her blessing whispered, Gloria took a big bite. The food reminded her of Paul's text. She reached into her purse and pulled out her cell phone.

There was a message. "I'll pick you up at 6 p.m. sharp." She texted a smiley face then set the phone down on the table.

"Paul's taking me to dinner," Gloria announced. She wasn't sure that Ruth had heard her. The earbuds were back in place.

But Ruth had heard. She nodded. Gloria made a mental note that Ruth's hearing was pretty sharp.

Ruth kept one eye on the monitor and looked up at Gloria with the other. "Steve Colby called a little while ago and asked me to dinner."

Gloria raised her eyebrows and took a bite of sandwich. So Slick Steve was interested in Ruth. Gloria did a mental scolding. She really needed to stop calling him Slick Steve. He was a nice guy and the nickname was a bad habit. "That's nice. Where's he taking you?"

The other eyeball was off the screen and both were focused on Gloria. Color crept into

Ruth's cheeks. "I don't know. He said it was a surprise. He told me he thought I could use a little cheering up."

Gloria nodded her approval. The more she got to know Steve Colby, the more she liked him. She pushed aside the small voice that told her he wanted to add Ruth as another notch on his belt...

Gloria spent the rest of the afternoon upstairs sorting through more stuff. She had finished sorting clothes and was now sifting through boxes of paperback books. She finished just in time to get ready for her date with Paul. She nodded her head in approval as she did a final walk-thru of the upstairs bedrooms. This was a project that had needed to be done years ago. No - decades ago.

She was proud of her accomplishment as she shut off the lights and headed downstairs. Her heart fluttered as she thought about seeing

Paul. It had been days now. It seemed even longer.

Gloria soaked her sore muscles in the tub. She'd sprinkled the water with rose scented bath oils. The smell of lilac was her favorite but roses came in a close second.

She fussed with her hair and makeup, then headed to her closet to pick out an outfit. She settled on a pair of black dress slacks and a pink blouse. She slipped a heart-shaped locket around her neck - the one that had all her children's birthstones framing the front. A quick splash of her favorite perfume on her wrists and neck and she was ready to go.

It was 5:30 now. She wandered into the kitchen. Ruth was in the exact same spot, staring at the computer screen. "You're going to burn your retina staring at that screen," Gloria kidded.

"Huh?" Ruth's head craned around.

"What time is Steve picking you up?" Gloria asked.

"Oh, around six," Ruth answered.

"It's already 5:30," Gloria pointed out.

Ruth's eyes shot up to the clock. "Oh my gosh!" She jumped out of the chair and ran from the room. Seconds later, Gloria could hear water running in the bathroom.

Gloria bent down and stared at the computer screen. She slipped into Ruth's chair and scooched it forward. The post office had been closed for half an hour now. What could Ruth possibly be looking at?

A movement in the right hand corner of the screen caught her eye. Someone was inside the post office. She squinted and leaned in for a closer look. The person's back was to the screen. Gloria couldn't make out who it was. Her eyes never left the monitor as she groped the kitchen table in search of her glasses. Her fingertips touched the frames and she slipped them on.

Whoever it was, was wearing dark clothes. The figure disappeared from view. She sat quiet as a mouse and watched. The figure reappeared from behind the mail slots then walked over to the monitor and stared directly into the camera.

Gloria gasped. Her hand shot up and she covered her mouth. It was Kenny! He looked right into the camera. Then he lifted his thumb and gave the camera the thumbs up!

Ruth knew Kenny was in the post office. Kenny knew about the camera!

The bathroom door handle rattled. Gloria jumped from the chair and ran out onto the porch. She didn't dare let on to Ruth that she had seen Kenny in front of the camera.

Gloria's heart began to pound. What did this mean? That Kenny and Ruth were working together? Were they the middle men in the drug ring? What other explanation could there be?

She paced the porch floor and watched as Mally raced across the gravel drive in hot pursuit of a squirrel. This was unbelievable! They say you never really know someone. But Ruth??

"Oh, there you are." Ruth poked her head out the porch door.

Gloria spun around to face her, a smile pasted on her face. "Just letting Mally run for a bit before Paul gets here," she said.

"Can I borrow some of your perfume?" Ruth asked.

Gloria nodded. "It's in on my bedroom dresser," she told her.

Ruth disappeared inside and Gloria turned back around. Just in time to see Paul pull in.

Gloria could barely wait for him to get out of the car. She met him at the car door and held out her arms. He slid out of the driver's seat, wrapped his arms around her and pulled her close. "You are a sight for sore eyes," he murmured into her hair.

Gloria blinked back tears. The week had been a rough one. And it was getting rougher by the minute. She breathed in. The scent of his cologne lingered on his shirt. It was one of her favorites. You smell nice and you feel even better," she told him.

He pulled back, just far enough to gaze into her eyes. "I was about to say the exact same thing." Paul looked up at the house. "Ruth here?"

She nodded. "Steve Colby asked her out to dinner. She's inside getting ready," she explained.

They wandered back to the porch and reached the top step at the same time Steve

Colby's car pulled in the drive. He parked on the other side, opposite Paul's vehicle.

They watched as he climbed from the car and headed over to where they were waiting. Steve had a bouquet of flowers in his hand.

Paul glanced down at Gloria and frowned. "I forgot to bring you flowers."

She squeezed his hand. "Really, you don't need to bring them every time."

Steve was all spiffed up in dark brown dress slacks and button-down shirt. His hair was slicked back and he was wearing cowboy boots.

Gloria smiled brightly. "How are you this evening, Steve?"

Steve grinned. "Doing great. And yourself?" He nodded at Paul.

"Just fine." She nodded towards the house. "I think Ruth's almost ready. Let me go check on her." She excused herself and walked back inside.

The first thing Gloria noticed when she stepped inside was that the laptop was gone. Ruth had put it away! Which was a bit odd. The thing had sat in the exact same spot since the moment Ruth brought it into the house!

She was convinced it was because she didn't want Gloria to see Kenny inside the post office! Gloria pushed the thought aside as Ruth stepped into the kitchen. She'd just have to deal with this later.

"You look nice," Gloria complimented her. And she did look nice. She had on a lovely pair of gray slacks and beaded black blouse. Her dangling earrings matched her shirt. She smelled nice, too.

"Thanks for letting me use your perfume," Ruth said. Her eyes darted to the porch door. "Is he here yet?"

Gloria nodded. "He's out on the porch talking to Paul."

Ruth bit her lower lip and tugged on the edge of her blouse.

Gloria could see she was nervous as a tic. "Here, we'll go out together," she told her. She grabbed Ruth's hand and pulled her across the kitchen and out to the porch. Poor Ruth's hand was cold and clammy.

Gloria whispered words of encouragement. "You'll have fun. Don't worry!"

Ruth nodded nervously and sucked in a breath before following Gloria outside.

Steve looked almost as nervous as Ruth! When he saw his date, he reached up and smoothed both sides of his hair back, then cleared his throat. He thrust the flowers in Ruth's direction. "These are for you."

At first, Ruth just stared at them. Then she stared at Steve. Then she stared back at the flowers. "For me?"

Gloria was uncomfortable for them both. "Let me go get a vase."

"They're beautiful!" Ruth took the flowers and pulled the bouquet to her face. "They smell wonderful." There was of mix of yellow roses, pink carnations and sprigs of lavender.

Paul and Gloria waited for Steve and Ruth to head out before Gloria locked the door and followed Paul to his car. "Ruth has a key?" Gloria nodded. She'd given her one the first night she got there. She trusted her friend implicitly. Or she had. Until just a few minutes ago...

"How are your houseguests?" Gloria remembered Paul's son, Jeff, and his wife, Tina.

Paul rubbed his forehead. "I don't know what's going to happen with those two. They don't seem to be in any hurry to move out."

"Maybe you're making them too comfortable?" she guessed.

He nodded. "That's what I'm afraid of." He glanced at Gloria in the passenger seat. "I'm trying to encourage them to start saving some money and look for a place of their own." He sighed heavily. "It's like talking to a brick wall."

Paul's plan was to one day leave the farm and everything he had to his son and daughter. But not yet. Not when he was still alive and living there! Plus, if Jeff and Tina stayed on, what would his daughter, Allie, think? The farm was part of her inheritance, too. What was that saying? *Possession is 9/10ths of the law.*

"How's it going with Ruth and the investigation?" He knew Gloria well enough to know she was doing her own detective work. He couldn't blame her on this one. He was sure

Gloria didn't mind having her friend stay with her, but if she was anything like him, she was ready for her life to return to normal.

"Okay. So far, so good," she said. "Of course, it's only been a few days."

She stared out the window and watched the farm fields go by. "I heard that they're close to making an arrest."

Paul nodded. He wasn't involved in this investigation. The FBI was thorough, though. If they were close to an arrest, their homework was almost done. Which meant soon Gloria's house guest would be gone.

Paul turned onto the road that led into Green Springs. "Where are you taking me?" she wondered.

He smiled. "A surprise. It's a new restaurant I discovered the other day when I was answering a call."

That was one perk to Paul's job. He found some nifty, out-of-the way places on his patrols. Places others didn't even know existed.

He drove through town and turned onto a small, two-lane road on the outskirts. The road twisted and turned for a few miles before a clearing came into view. Straight ahead of them was a small lake. Off to the left, a small chalet-style restaurant.

He pulled the car into the paved parking lot. She grabbed the door handle to climb out.

He reached out and touched her arm. "Uh-uh! Let me be a gentlemen."

Gloria took her hand off the handle and waited while he came around to open her door. She put her hand in his and he helped her out. On impulse, he bent down and kissed her. "I've been waiting to do that for days now!"

Instead of walking in the front door, he led her down a path that ran along the side of the

144

building and to the back. A long, wooden walkway opened out onto a larger, more expansive deck that overlooked the lake.

A tropical tiki bar filled up one side of the balcony area. Beside the bar area, a lone musician strummed his guitar.

The patio wasn't even half-full yet. They settled into a table for two near the railing, which had a spectacular view of the lake. The lake was like a sheet of glass.

The waitress took their drink order and left them to stare out at the calm waters. It was nice to be together. It was nice to be alone. The irony that both of them were there not only to be together but to get a break from their houseguests didn't escape either of them.

Paul dragged his eyes from the serene view and gazed across the table at Gloria. "What's your take on the investigation down at the post office?"

Gloria had to wait to answer. The waitress had returned with their drinks and a bowl of chips and salsa.

"Not only has Ruth been put on leave, Kenny, the route carrier, was put on leave, too."

Paul plucked a chip from the bowl and dipped it in the salsa. "Didn't you say they thought it was an inside job?"

Gloria nodded. "Yeah. The only one still working is the part-timer, Seth."

Paul raised his eyebrows. "Oh? What does he do?"

Gloria explained how his job was to load the boxes on the trucks that were headed for the airport. "He's in college and works three or four afternoons during the week," she explained.

She didn't mention the fact that Ruth had installed surveillance equipment and how Gloria had seen Kenny on the monitor, signaling to

Ruth just a few hours earlier. Gloria wanted time to mull that piece of information over first.

Kenny – and Ruth – could get into a whole heap of trouble if they were caught inside the post office after being banned. And what was Kenny doing? Obviously, Ruth knew Kenny was in there. The fact that he stood right in front of the camera and signaled her was a dead giveaway. Should she confront Ruth? Or maybe Kenny?

"Earth to Gloria..." Paul snapped his fingers in front of her face.

She jerked her head and grimaced. "Not much of a date tonight, huh," she said.

Paul sighed heavily. "Me neither." He shook his head. "What do you think I should do about the kids? Give them a deadline? Tell them they need to move out and risk alienating them?"

Paul had a bigger dilemma than Gloria. After all, Ruth would move out. Eventually. Hopefully soon...

Paul was in a tough spot. What would Gloria do if one of her kids moved in? It would depend on the circumstances. The plan. But it sounded like the only plan these two had was to stay right where they were...

"Maybe sit down and explain to them that it's not fair to Allie to let them stay forever. After all, someday half that house will be hers." Gloria paused. "What *does* Allie think of all this?"

The food arrived just then. They waited for the waitress to leave before Paul answered. "So far she's okay with it. But Allie has a strong personality and she'll only put up with it for so long." He smiled. "If she thinks they're taking advantage of me, she'll get onto them."

Gloria stabbed a fork full of chicken and lettuce. "Maybe you should let it ride and let Allie handle it when the time comes." She chewed thoughtfully for several seconds. "Or better yet, call a family meeting. You know, Allie, Jeff and Tina. Put it out there as a meeting to help figure out how they can get back on track and on their feet again."

She pointed the tines of her fork at Paul. "Yes, I think that would be the best idea. Head this off before it becomes a much bigger problem."

Paul nodded. "That's what I love about you! You're my little problem-solver!"

He cut off a slice of pork chop and held it out to Gloria. "You have to try this. It is so good!"

She opened her mouth and let him feed her from his fork. It was delicious. She made a mental note to experiment now that she knew how much he loved pork chops. "Delicious," she mumbled.

Paul lifted his water glass and took a sip before peering at her over the edge. "How about if you come for the family meeting, too? You know, a sort of referee!"

Gloria was already shaking her head. She was anxious to meet Paul's children but that wasn't the way to do it. "Nice try, but I think I'll wait until this blows over before I meet your kids."

The sun had dipped down over the lake. The yellow glow on the water was soft and soothing. Gloria glanced down at her plate. She was full and had only eaten about half the food. She loaded her leftovers in a to-go container and they wandered back out to the parking lot.

The evening had flown by. She frowned when she realized she couldn't even invite him in for coffee or dessert! Unless, of course, Ruth wasn't back yet.

But Ruth was back. The kitchen lights were on. The blinds were open and she could see

Ruth sitting at the kitchen table staring at the computer screen!

Paul's face fell. "I guess you won't be inviting me in for dessert," he said.

"Sure! C'mon in! It'll just be the three of us!" She snapped her fingers. "Hey! I have an idea! Why don't we move Ruth in with your kids and then we'll have a place to ourselves."

Paul glanced at her out of the corner of his eye and then leaned across the driver's seat. "You mean shack up?"

Gloria slapped his arm. "No!" Her face turned red. "You know that's not what I meant," she sputtered.

She giggled as she envisioned telling her family and friends that she and Paul were moving in together. Not that they ever would unless they were married. Still, visualizing the expressions on their faces made her grin.

"Aha! You *are* thinking about it," he teased.

Gloria narrowed her eyes and crossed her arms in front of her. "Paul Kennedy, you know that's not true!"

Paul unbuckled his seatbelt. He leaned over to the passenger side and slid his arm around her shoulders. He pulled her close and whispered in her ear. "Yeah, but what if we eloped?"

She giggled. Now that would make the tongues in Belhaven wag! She reached over and put her hand on the back of his head and pulled him close. "Convince me that we should," she flirted.

He tipped his head and touched his lips to hers. It was a sweet, warm kiss. It almost reminded her of when she would go on a date as a teenager and her parents were awake and waiting for her inside at the end of a date.

Paul read her mind. "This date night and kissing in the car makes me feel like a teenager again," he said.

Gloria peeked around Paul's head. She could see Ruth's face turned toward the driveway. She let out a deep sigh. "I better go before she comes out here and starts tapping on the window, wondering if we're okay."

Gloria grabbed the door handle and started to pull. "Let me know how the family meeting turns out," she said.

The light mood was over at the thought of confronting his grown children. It was something he wasn't looking forward to, but knew it was something that had to be done. Before they got too comfy.

He watched as Gloria made her way up the steps and opened the porch door. She turned around and blew him a kiss before disappearing inside the house.

Chapter 5

Gloria woke unusually early the next morning. She lay there in bed wondering what on earth had woken her. She glanced at the clock. It was 6:30 a.m. and still dark outside.

A light *tap tap* interrupted her thoughts. The tapping noise was the rattling of pipes. Water pipes. Which mean only one thing. Ruth was already up.

Gloria was up most mornings before Ruth, but not today. That meant only one thing. Gloria had a hunch Ruth was up to something. She flung her feet over the edge of the bed and slipped her feet into her slippers. She pulled her bathrobe on and wandered into the other room. A bright light shone under the bathroom door. She could hear water running in the bathroom sink.

She shuffled past the door and into the kitchen, which was still dark. Gloria flipped on the light switch. Mally opened one eye and stared up at Gloria as if to say, *what on earth are you doing?* Even she knew it was too early. She closed her eyes and sighed before rolling over and burying her head between the wall and her doggie bed.

Coffee. Gloria needed coffee. She started the pot and pulled out a kitchen chair. She could see the newspaper lying on the porch. She wandered out and grabbed the paper.

When she stepped back in the kitchen, she ran right into Ruth, who was fully dressed. She looked as if she was leaving. Or, better yet, sneaking out.

She stopped abruptly when she spied Gloria. "Oh! Uh. I was just going to leave you a note. I couldn't sleep and for some reason was worried about the house. You know, like I needed to check on it," she explained.

Gloria didn't buy it. Not for a minute. She wondered if this had something to do with Kenny sneaking into the post office the night before. Her eyes narrowed. *Was she going to meet Kenny?*

She had a strong hunch that was exactly what she planned to do. "Oh. Okay." Gloria poured a cup of coffee, then wandered over to the kitchen table to have a seat. Like she didn't care at all that Ruth was leaving the house before daylight to check on a house she hadn't been the least bit worried about. Until now.

"How was the date with Steve?"

Ruth stopped at the door. She glanced at the flowers centered on the table and turned a pale shade of pink. "It was very nice," she said. "We might go out again."

Gloria nodded. "You want a cup of coffee before you go?" she asked.

Ruth looked at the coffee pot and shook her head. "No. I think I'll stop by Dot's after I check on the place," she said.

Gloria nodded, then grabbed the paper and began to read the front page, all the while watching Ruth out of the corner of her eye.

Ruth paused for a moment, as if she might change her mind. That didn't last long. She grabbed the door handle and opened it. "I'll see you later," she said.

Gloria nodded. "Okay." She didn't look up from her paper as Ruth shut the door behind her and headed down the steps.

Gloria crept out of the chair and made her way over to the kitchen window. She peeked around the edge of the frame and stared at Ruth's back as she headed to her van.

When Ruth climbed in the driver's seat, Gloria darted out of the kitchen and ran to her bedroom. There was no time for a shower. No time to brush her teeth. She was determined to find out what Ruth was up to!

She blindly reached into her closet and pulled out the first thing her hand came in contact with. A pair of dark blue sweatpants and a t-shirt she'd picked up in Chicago the summer before when she'd visited her son, Eddie, and his wife, Karen. It had a picture of the old Sears Tower on it. Of course, it wasn't called Sears Tower anymore. It had another name.

She yanked on the sweat pants and pulled the shirt over her head, then bolted back into the kitchen. She slipped on a pair of sandals by the door, grabbed her purse off the kitchen chair and her keys before she bolted out the door.

Gloria had a sneaking suspicion that Ruth was not going to meet Kenny at her house. There were too many neighbors close by. No. She was headed to Kenny's place out in the country where no one could spy on them. No one that is, except Gloria.

She threw her purse on the passenger seat and fired up the engine. She backed up and turned the wheel, then pulled forward. She roared out of the driveway and toward Kenny's place. Her adrenaline was pumping as she pressed down on the gas pedal and exceeded the speed limit. Just a little.

She had just a few short minutes to figure out *how* she could spy on Ruth and Kenny and not have her cover blown. Then she remembered the field that ran parallel to Kenny's place. There was a small two-lane dirt path the tractors used to get to the fields. A wooden fence ran alongside it.

She pulled into the path and coasted down the rutted trail. Her car bounced up and down as she tried to ease in far enough so she wouldn't be spotted from the road. From her vantage point in the car, she couldn't see much. Actually, she couldn't see anything. She slid out of the car and gently eased the door shut.

Gloria ducked down as she tiptoed along the tree line. She looked down at her outfit. At least her clothes were dark! She moved far enough along so that she could see both the back of Kenny's house and the driveway. Her heart sank when she spied the empty drive. Ruth wasn't here! Neither was Kenny!

Maybe they were over at Ruth's place after all! She turned to head back to the car when she saw bright headlights beam through the row of trees. Gloria stiffened straight up and plastered herself against the nearest tree.

The lights shut off and so did the car's engine. A door slammed. Another beam of light flashed around the tree.

Beads of sweat covered Gloria's brow and her heart began to pound in her chest. Had she been spotted? She closed her eyes and began to pray. Maybe this wasn't such a great idea after all!

The beam of light disappeared and was followed by the distinct sound of another door slamming. Muffled voices echoed through the trees. Gloria slid down to the ground and turned around. She peeked around the side of the tree.

Two figures stood underneath the bright porch light. It was Ruth and Kenny! They were bent close together, talking in low voices. Ruth would pause every couple of seconds and glance behind her, as if waiting for someone else.

"...come in...." The words wafted through the trees. Ruth shook her head. Kenny headed up the porch steps and disappeared inside his house. He reappeared a few moments later, a box in his hand. He handed the box to Ruth.

Gloria watched as she opened the box and stuck her hand inside. Satisfied with whatever the contents were, she gave Kenny a quick hug then climbed back into her car.

Kenny watched as Ruth pulled out of the drive before he stepped back inside his house.

Could it be that whatever was in the box was what Kenny had snuck into the post office the night before to get? Gloria had a hunch that was exactly what it was.

Gloria jogged back to her car. Well, not really jogged since she was wearing flip-flops. She shuffled across the wet weeds to get back to her car. She wondered if Ruth would bring the box back to Gloria's place. Or maybe she would she drop it off at her own house?

She climbed into Anabelle and headed back towards town. She turned the car down the street that ran opposite Ruth's tidy ranch. She peered between the houses and could see Ruth's van parked in the drive. Gloria drove around the block as she waited for Ruth to leave. The third drive around the block was the charm. Ruth's van was gone.

Gloria turned onto her street. She pulled into the driveway and put the car in park. *Should she or shouldn't she? What if Ruth came back and caught Gloria inside her house? Even if she did, she was pretty confident that Ruth wouldn't press charges.*

As much as Gloria wanted to get inside and look for the box, she could envision this ending badly for her. If Ruth caught her, at the very least it could put an end to their friendship.

It wasn't worth the risk. Gloria put Anabelle in reverse and slowly backed out of the drive. Whatever Ruth was up to, there had to be a logical explanation. After all, Ruth couldn't really be a drug lord, could she?

Gloria passed Dot's restaurant on her way back to the farm. She drove right by Ruth's van, which was parked out front.

When she got home, she let Mally out before she headed to the shower. She lathered up her hair and mulled over what information she did have.

So far, nothing made sense. Obviously, whoever had been in the dumpster the other night was not part of Ruth's little group. Maybe it was a homeless person rummaging through the bins looking for something of value. She dismissed the thought. She had never spotted a homeless person in their small town of Belhaven before.

Then Gloria had another thought. What about the person that broke into Andrea's place? Did that have some sort of connection to the drug trafficking?

She decided a stop by Andrea's was in order. She could check on her friend and find out if any other odd occurrences had happened.

She passed Ruth on her way to Andrea's and waved. They were like two ships passing in the night. Or in this case, in the day.

Andrea's car was the only one in the drive when she pulled in. There was no contractor trucks or vans. She made her way to the front door and reached for the bell. Instead of a bell, there was a brand spanking-new nifty door knocker. It was in the shape of a lion's head. She grinned and grabbed the ring. She gave it three loud taps and waited.

Seconds later, Andrea swung the door open. She was dressed in what Gloria would term as garden gear. She had a red bandanna tied across her head. Her shorts were splattered with paint and her t-shirt was a rainbow of colors.

Andrea grabbed Gloria's hand and pulled her in. "You must have ESP. I was just going to call you!"

"Follow me." She didn't wait for Gloria to answer. Instead, she grabbed the mahogany handrail and climbed the steps to the second floor.

Andrea had been taunting Gloria for weeks now about some sort of surprise. Something she'd been working on that she didn't want Gloria to see until it was finished.

Brutus followed them up the steps. Gloria had forgotten all about Andrea's new companion. "Well, hello there my furry friend."

Brutus stuck his head under her hand and thumped his tail. "I bet you know all about the surprise, don't you?" The dog and Gloria trailed Andrea up the grand staircase.

At the top of the stairs, Andrea turned left, in the direction of the master suite. She swung the double doors open and stood to the side. Her face beamed with pride.

Gloria couldn't remember the last time she'd been in Andrea's bedroom. It might have been the night the Blackstone brothers had kidnapped them. Or maybe it was the night Gloria and Lucy snuck in the house and found the stolen money in the floorboards. She glanced at the spot where she and Lucy had uncovered the cash.

She had never mentioned the discovery to Andrea. Of course, Andrea hadn't owned the house at the time they found the money...

Gloria gasped at her first look around the room. It was stunning and it looked so different. The room looked bigger somehow. If that was possible.

"Well, what do you think?" Andrea asked.

"This is a room fit for a princess," Gloria said.

The walls were painted a muted gray. The trim bright white. New plantation shutters covered all the bedroom windows. The exterior of the fireplace had been redone in a sleek, blue slate. Two pale, purple wingback chairs faced the fireplace. Wide plank wooden floors completed the look.

Still, something was different about the room. Gloria stuck her hand on her hip and spun around.

Andrea grinned. She knew Gloria couldn't figure out what the big change was. "It's the ceilings." She lifted an index finger and pointed up.

Gloria focused her gaze on the ceiling. "Well, I'll be. You're right!" The ceiling had once been low and flat. They were now cathedral ceilings with interesting lines. A small, cozy window nook was tucked in one corner of the room. A sparkling chandelier hung over the massive, king-size bed.

She motioned Gloria to the bathroom. "That's not all." Andrea pressed on the side wall - the secret entrance to the master bath. She hit the light switch and stepped inside. The original marble tile that surrounded the tub had been polished, and the tub itself had been replaced. It was a bit bigger than the original and this one was jetted. Stained-glass windows surrounded the tub on three sides and a crystal chandelier sparkled from above.

The marble on the double vanity had also been polished. Brand new, sleek, modern sinks and faucets had been installed. Small storage cabinets had been installed on both sides of the vanity. Crown molding gave the ceiling a touch of elegance.

Gloria walked over and skimmed her hand across the gleaming marble top. "This is almost too pretty to use."

Andrea wandered to the door on the other side of the bath. "Check out the closet."

There was no light switch to flip in this room. Instead, it was all motion sensor. They stepped inside and recessed lights instantly brightened the interior. Custom shelves and cabinets lined the walls. There was a whole section devoted to shoes. It was jam-packed.

Gloria gazed down at the collection. "I never knew you liked shoes that much."

"It's my downfall," Andrea confessed. "I love shoes." She went on. "But, hey, you'll never guess what the workers found when they were redoing this closet."

She stepped over to the corner. The one with the built-in cabinet. "Check this out," Andrea said.

She stuck her hand under the cabinet. The cabinet glided seamlessly backwards and stopped a few feet in. Andrea reached around the corner. A bright light came on and revealed a secret room!

Gloria leaned forward and peeked through the narrow opening.

"Follow me." Andrea turned sideways and squeezed in through the small space. Gloria followed her in. She glanced down at the wall and her stomach that touched the frame. Too many more desserts and she'd get stuck!

The room wasn't large. Maybe six feet by nine feet. The walls were smooth concrete. A small, plaid sofa sat in the corner. An end table with a small lamp sat beside it. There were two TV monitors on one of the walls.

Andrea pressed the button on one of the monitors. A view of the front door appeared.

Gloria placed a hand on the smooth concrete and stared at the screen. "You have a panic room," she said.

"I know, right? I ordered a safe to put in here."

Andrea stuck her finger on the power button to turn off the screen when a figure appeared at the front door. It was Brian. "We better go down," she said.

She flipped off the light and Gloria followed her out of the closet, then out of the bedroom. "How many people know about that room?"

Andrea counted with her fingers. "You, the contractor, one of the workers," she got to the fourth finger, "and me."

Andrea gave her a dark glance. "I was thinking maybe I should keep it that way," she said.

Gloria nodded. "I agree 100%! By the way, have you had any more people wandering around or odd occurrences?"

They were on the stairs now and could hear the *thump thump* of Andrea's newly-installed knocker. Andrea shook her head. "Nope, thank goodness."

The smile never left Brian's face when Andrea opened the door to let him in the foyer. "Well, well. Two of favorite girls." He kissed Andrea's forehead and then hugged Gloria. "I've been thinking about you," Brian said.

"Oh yeah?"

"Wondering if your washer was still working and if your houseguest was still there. I'm gonna go out on a limb and say the answer to both is yes?" His eyebrows raised.

Gloria's shoulders slumped – just a little. Andrea had taken Gloria's mind off her troubles, but they were back now in full force. "Yeah. Any news on the post office investigation?"

If anyone would have info, it would be Brian since he had a lot of people come in and out of the hardware store every day. He shook his head. "Nope. Not a peep. They're keeping a tight lid on it over there," he said.

"You want to join us for lunch?" Andrea asked.

Gloria shook her head. "No. I have another stop to make before I head back home. Maybe next time." She hugged Andrea and Brian and headed to the car.

It was time to stop by her friend, Lucy's, place. She hadn't seen much of her lately. Just briefly when she came by the farm to drop off a load for the yard sale.

Lucy's jeep was in the drive. Gloria pulled in beside it. She started for the porch door when she heard a muffled voice. "Over here!"

Gloria rounded the end of the house and circled the bush on the edge of Lucy's garden. Lucy was bent over a tomato plant. A bushel basket rested on her hip. She straightened her back and shaded her eyes with her free hand. "My, my. If it isn't my long-lost best friend," she said wryly.

Gloria defended herself. "You know I've been busy."

Lucy tip-toed past the tidy rows of plants and over to where Gloria was standing. "I know. I'm just teasing..." She set the basket on the grass and motioned Gloria towards the house. "How's it going with the houseguest?"

"Ruth's fine. No problem at all," Gloria answered. She remembered her date last night with Paul. "It is cramping my style a little," she admitted.

Lucy was on the top step now. She spun around. "Oh yeah? What style is that?"

"You know. Dates. Stuff like that," she added.

"So go over to Paul's place," Lucy logically suggested. She held the door for Gloria to go inside.

"We would but Paul's kids just moved in," she said.

Lucy snorted. "You don't say."

Gloria pulled out a kitchen chair and sat down. She stuck her chin in her fist. "Yeah. I do say."

Lucy headed to the kitchen sink. She scrubbed the dirt and grime off her hands then wiped them on a towel hanging on the side of the fridge. "Have you eaten lunch yet?"

Gloria's stomach grumbled in response. "Nope."

Lucy reached into the fridge and pulled out a box of fried chicken. "Good. You can help me with this."

She reached in and pulled out a container of coleslaw and another one with potato salad. She set them on the table and grabbed a pitcher of iced tea.

"Here, let me do something." Gloria jumped to her feet and helped set the table. The two loaded their plates, then said their blessing. The chicken was delicious, even cold.

"Did you get this from Dot's place?" Gloria asked. She peeled off a piece of white meat and popped it into her mouth.

Lucy nodded. "Yeah. She's trying a new recipe and asked if I wanted to be the guinea pig."

The meat was moist and tender, the coating nice and crispy and seasoned with the right amount of salt. Gloria made a mental note to tell Dot it was delicious.

Lucy reached for a drumstick. "Any news on the investigation?"

Gloria shook her head. "Brian said the investigators are keeping a tight lid on the case." She hesitated for a fraction of a second. Should she tell Lucy about Ruth? She decided she needed a second opinion. Lucy had helped her out with other investigations. Maybe they could put their heads together...

Gloria set her half-eaten piece of chicken down and took a deep breath. Gloria told her everything that had happened so far.

Lucy's eyes widened when she told her how Ruth had surveillance equipment inside the post office. "Can't she get in trouble for that?"

"That's what I thought, too." Gloria pointed at her own chest. "But I'm not going to say anything."

Lucy shook her head and made a locking motion in front of her lips. "Me either."

Gloria went on to tell Lucy how she caught a glimpse of Kenny in front of the camera the night before and how she followed Ruth to Kenny's that morning and watched as he handed Ruth a box.

Lucy stopped chewing and gasped. "What do you think is in the box?"

"I wish I knew," she said. I thought about taking a peek in the bedroom when she's not around," Gloria confessed. "You know, to see if the box is in there."

Lucy nodded. Her red head bounced up and down. "Good idea. After all, it is your house," she pointed out.

Lucy tossed the empty container of coleslaw and potato salad in the trash. She put the rest of the chicken back in the fridge and pulled out a baker's box. Inside was a lemon meringue pie.

Gloria's mouth watered. "Did Dot give that to you, too?"

Lucy pulled the lid off and lifted the pie from the box. "Yep. She wanted me to run this by my taste buds. She's thinking about adding this to the menu, too."

"Why doesn't she ever ask me to taste test for her?" Gloria complained.

Lucy sliced a generous piece and set it on a plate in front of Gloria. "Cuz you're never around?"

"True..." Gloria cut off the tip with her fork and put it in her mouth. The meringue was just the right thickness. The lemon was tart with a hint of sweet and the crust flaky - yet firm. "This would be a home run," she declared.

Lucy wiped the meringue off with a napkin before taking a bite.

"You don't like meringue?" Gloria asked. She had never known Lucy to not like a sweet.

Lucy nodded. "Yep. Believe it or not, I'm not a fan of meringue." She took another bite. "But lemon pie, now that's another story."

Gloria stayed long enough for a second glass of tea before she decided it was time to go.

Lucy walked her to the car. She watched as Gloria opened the door and slid inside. "Maybe you should confront Ruth. Tell her what you saw..."

Gloria nodded. "I was thinking the same thing. I mean, what could she really have to hide?"

Chapter 6

Gloria grabbed the mail out of the mailbox on her way to the house. She flipped through the pile. Nothing but junk mail and bills.

The roar of a car racing past the farm caught Gloria's attention. She looked up just in time to catch a glimpse of a four-door sedan with tinted windows speed by. It was navy blue. The same color as Detective Sharon McIntyre's car. *Now what's she doing way out here?* Gloria wondered.

Gloria wandered into the house, dropped her mail on the counter and her purse on a chair.

Her cell phone chirped, letting her know there was a message. She popped on her reading glasses and picked up the phone. *Meet me out at the flea market at 1 p.m. sharp. I have some information on the post office investigation.*

Gloria didn't recognize the number. It wasn't someone she had programmed in her phone. But it was a local number. She glanced at the clock. It was already 12:45.

She let out an aggravated sigh. It would take ten minutes just to get there. She grabbed her purse and shoved the phone inside.

Mally thumped her tail and let out a low whine. Gloria looked at the furry face. "C'mon, girl. You can be my guard dog."

Mally scrambled to her feet and met Gloria at the door. The two of them climbed into Anabelle and hit the road. There were two ways to get to the flea market. Straight into town until the street ended and then turn left OR turn left and go through town with one right turn. Either way would take about the same time to get there. Gloria decided on the drive-through-town route. That way, she could see if Ruth was still at Dot's place.

She was. Her car was parked in the same spot.

She made the right at the end of main street and towards the flea market grounds. The flea market was open only on Mondays. The place would be like a ghost town today.

She passed the first block, then the second block. The third block ended at one of the entrances to the grounds. There was one lone car parked in front of the animal auction building. The car belonged to Judith Arnett!

Judith was Belhaven's unofficial troublemaker and gossip extraordinaire. She and a few of her cronies spent most of their time slandering others and spreading vicious rumors. Not long ago, Judith had tried to steal a small espresso machine from Dot's restaurant and Dot had banned her from the restaurant for life.

Gloria wasn't much of a fan. It was best to avoid some people and in Gloria's book, Judith was one of them.

Gloria pulled Anabelle into the empty spot next to Judith's car. She glanced over at Judith's car. It was empty.

Gloria and Mally climbed out of Anabelle and shuffled across the hard-packed dirt to the open side of the auctioneer's building.

Judith was standing in the shadow of the lean-to, hidden from the street. "You're right on time," she said.

Gloria nodded. "You said you had some information on the post office investigation."

Judith glanced around, as if someone might be nearby and eavesdrop on their conversation. She lowered her voice. "I kind of got this by accident. Yesterday, I was headed down the alley, the one that connects main street to the road that the old school's on."

"Yes, I know the one."

"Anyways, I was headed from Mary's place back to my car." Mary was one of the gals in

185

Judith's small circle. "That's when I saw Sharon, the detective lady. She was bent over, talking to someone inside a car."

"Did you recognize the car?" Gloria asked.

"Nope," Judith said. "I knew something was up so I flattened myself to the side of the fence. I couldn't hear what they were saying but I was able to peek through an opening in the fence and I had a clear view of them. Suddenly, the person in the car handed the detective this!"

Judith whipped out her cell phone and turned the screen on. She tapped the surface and handed it to Gloria. Gloria slid her reading glasses on and studied the screen. It was a picture of the detective taking a white box from whoever was in the car. A white box that looked a lot like the one Ruth had picked up from Kenny that morning!

Gloria stared at the arm. It was long and a bit on the scrawny side. She looked up. "Can you forward a copy of that picture to me?"

Judith stared at the phone in her hand. "I would, but I don't know how," she confessed. She held the phone out to Gloria.

Gloria wasn't too familiar with the workings of the newer phones but she could try to figure it out. Much to her surprise, she pushed a few buttons on the screen and Voila! It worked!

Judith scrunched up her eyes. "How'd you do that? I've had this phone for months now and could never figure that out."

Gloria held the phone out, then showed her how to send a picture. Judith's face lit up when Gloria was done. "Now I can send some pictures to the grandkids."

Judith was a lot like the other women in town, including Gloria herself. Her kids – and grandkids – lived hundreds, if not thousands of miles away. "Thanks, Gloria!"

Gloria smiled. "Thank *you* for your sharp eye and for sharing this with me."

"Do you think it means anything?" Judith asked. Gloria knew Judith was trying to help. Ruth wasn't one of her "cronies," but the two of them were friends.

Gloria nodded. "It might. I wish I knew what was in that box."

Judith nodded. "Yeah, if we knew what was in the box, it might help, huh."

They headed back to their cars. Mally trailed behind.

"We need to get Ruth back to work," Judith said. "Looks like I'll need to keep a closer eye on the goings-on behind the post office."

Gloria patted her arm. "I need all the help I can get on this investigation," she admitted.

"I'm on it," Judith promised.

Gloria watched as Judith climbed into her car and drove off. She turned to Mally. "Now that is the most unlikely crime-solving partner I will ever have!"

She slid into the driver's seat and pulled her cell phone from her purse. She pulled up the phone number and added Judith Arnett to her contact list, certain that it would only be a matter of time before Judith contacted her again.

On the drive home, Gloria went over what she knew so far. What she knew so far pointed right to Ruth. Or maybe it was Ruth and Kenny. But what was the person in the car giving the detective? What in the world was in those boxes? Drugs? Money? Was Ruth turning a blind eye to illegal drug trafficking in exchange for cash?

Gloria shook her head. If she was, she sure didn't show it. Ruth had lived in the same house for years now. Her van was almost a decade old. She didn't dress in expensive clothes or wear lots of jewelry.

Gloria sucked in her breath. Her eyes flew open. *Or – what if Ruth had a drug problem?*

Ruth's van was in the drive when Gloria got home. She pulled in beside her and made her way up the steps. Ruth was in her usual spot. Glued to the computer screen. She looked up, then gave Gloria a small smile before staring at the screen again.

Gloria pulled out a chair and gazed at her friend. She tried to remember everything she had ever heard about drug use. Wasn't there something about dilated pupils? "So where did you and Steve go on your date?"

Ruth's gaze never left the screen. "We had a nice dinner over at that restaurant on the lake going into Lakeville."

"Do you think you'll go out again?" Gloria continued the conversation.

"Yeah, I think so," Ruth answered. "He's got a great sense of humor."

Gloria didn't know Steve that well. Only that he had left a trail of broken hearts in Belhaven. "How are you doing on sorting through stuff for the sale?"

"Good. I think I'm almost done," Ruth replied.

Gloria was growing impatient. Ruth was mesmerized by the stupid screen! She got up from her chair and plopped down in the one directly across from Ruth. She would have to at least glance up. "Will you be here for dinner?"

No answer.

Gloria snapped her fingers. "Hey!"

Ruth's blue-gray eyes shot up. They looked straight into Gloria's, then right back at the screen. It was not enough time for Gloria to determine whether or not her pupils were dilated!

She left Ruth at the table and headed to the bathroom. She switched on the light and studied her own pupils for something to compare it to. Hmm. Hers seemed to be medium dilated.

She wandered over to her own computer and fired it up. Then she typed in *signs of drug abuse.* She glanced over her shoulder. Ruth was like a stone statue.

She clicked on one of the tabs that listed some of the symptoms. The lists went on and on. How was she supposed to know if Ruth had any of these symptoms? Gloria herself had half the symptoms and she didn't even take drugs! Difficulty concentrating or remembering things, insomnia, increased appetite.... *Wasn't there something about having the munchies?*

Gloria clicked away from the screen and jumped out of the chair. She pulled a bag of chips from the kitchen pantry and set them on the table. "I think I'm going to have a snack. You want one?"

Ruth looked up. "Yeah. Something salty sounds good," she answered.

Gloria scooped a bunch of chips into a bowl and pushed it in Ruth's direction. Ruth munched on the chips and stared at the screen. Gloria put some in a bowl for herself. "Find anything new out?"

"Yeah! I'm going to have a mess on my hands when I get back there," she said. She shook her head. "They have no idea what they're doing. Why, I wouldn't be surprised if half the mail is being delivered to the wrong places!"

Gloria had to agree. Ruth ran a tight ship down at the post office.

Gloria picked up a chip. "I wonder how Kenny's holding up." She held her breath and waited to see if Ruth would mention seeing him that morning.

Ruth backed away from the monitor and leaned back in the chair. "I bet he's hating it. Just like me."

Gloria looked at Ruth. Really looked at her face. She looked tired. The dark circles under her eyes were something Gloria wasn't used to seeing. She was normally upbeat, peppy, a real chatterbox.

Gloria pushed her chair from the table and stood up. "Come on. We're going for a walk."

Ruth started to shake her head. "No. I need to keep watch."

Gloria stuck her hand on her hip and shook her finger at Ruth. "You need a break from this whole thing. Some fresh air will do you wonders."

She didn't wait for an answer. She snapped her fingers. "Let's go, Mally."

Gloria didn't have to ask Mally twice. She loved walks. Through the fields and the woods. She especially loved it when they walked all the way down to the stream, which was on the back side of the property.

Ruth reluctantly got out of her chair. "I suppose." She stared longingly at the screen.

Gloria reached over and flipped it shut. "It'll be there when you get back." She lifted a sweater from the hook and pulled it on. The skies were overcast and there was a bit of a chill in the air.

Ruth followed suit and grabbed her sweater from the back of the chair. Mally led the way as she bounded down the steps and circled the big oak tree beside the garden several times. The fields had been tilled and crops planted a while back. There was a grassy path that led down the center of the fields and to the woods.

Ruth stared at the tidy rows of crops. "What do you suppose they planted?" Sometimes Gloria could tell right away, but sometimes she had to wait until the tender plants peeked out from beneath the soil. Gloria bent down to examine one of the plants. "Those are beans."

Ruth nodded. She'd never gotten much into the farming aspect of living in a small, rural town. She'd grown up more of a city girl and had moved to Belhaven when she got the job as head postmaster. Before that, she'd worked as a mail clerk right out of high school where she worked her way up the ladder.

Mally was in the lead. She would stop every once in a while and take a step off the path. Gloria knew she was itching to run through the crops. She'd put one paw on the rich, dark soil to test Gloria and Gloria would warn her. "No, Mally." Then, she'd pull her paw back and continue on the grassy section.

The line of trees was in view now. It was a mini oasis at the end of the straight, flat fields. Years ago, James had told her that the original town of Belhaven was first settled out here. That there had been a small train depot, a few shops and several small houses beyond that.

That's what James's grandparents had told him. The only thing left of the structures now were a few spots where stones had been lined up, as if at one time they had been the foundations of the long-gone buildings.

The girls stepped into the small forest and the temperature dropped. A faint gurgling noise echoed through the trees. Gloria and Mally had been back here several times already this year. Mally knew right where she was going. She darted off into the woods and disappeared from sight.

Gloria followed behind and Ruth brought up the rear. Mally was drinking from the small stream when the girls caught up. Gloria sat on the edge of a nearby fallen tree, her usual resting spot when she and Mally came back here.

Ruth settled in next to her. She stared at the cool, clear water. "You don't think I'll lose my job, do you?" She turned to Gloria, tears threatening to spill down her cheeks.

Gloria grabbed her friend's hand and squeezed. She didn't know what to say, so she did the only thing that helped when life got her down and things seemed to be spinning out of control. "Let's pray about it."

Ruth nodded and the women bowed their heads. "Dear Lord, we pray for Ruth and her job. Lord, you know her heart. You know how much her job means to her. We ask that the investigators finish the investigation quickly so Ruth can get back to work. Thank you for your Son, our Savior, Jesus. In His name we pray. Amen."

The tear that had threatened now trailed down her cheeks. Ruth wiped them away with the back of her hand. "I feel better already," she whispered.

Mally was back now. She ended the somber moment when she shook her body and pelted the girls with droplets of cold water. "Oh, no!" Ruth screamed as she jumped up from the log.

The sun was sinking low in the sky by the time the girls wandered back across the fields and into Gloria's backyard. "The walk sure did help, Gloria. Thanks for making me go with you," Ruth said.

"You're welcome, my dear." Gloria opened the door and waited for Ruth to go in. "Tomorrow we can start organizing for the yard sale." The sale was creeping up on them. They had just a couple days left. "We should get together with the others and start pulling this thing together."

Ruth surprised Gloria when she walked over to the kitchen table, shut the lid on the laptop and then carried it off to her bedroom.

The phone on the wall rang at the same time Gloria opened the fridge to decide what to have for dinner. It was her daughter, Jill. Gloria had called her daughter the day before to see if she had anything she wanted to add to the yard sale.

"Hi, Jill."

"Hi, Mom. I went through a bunch of the boys stuff and have some clothes and toys I'd like to bring over."

"Sure. Ruth and I are going to organize tomorrow."

"Greg's working late tonight. The boys and I thought we'd stop over with a load and bring dinner with us if that's okay."

Gloria still had the fridge door open and it was slim pickins' inside. "That sounds great!"

"Was that Jill?" Ruth was back in the kitchen.

Gloria disconnected the line and set the phone back on the base. "Yeah. She and the boys are on their way with dinner. She wants to drop off some stuff for the yard sale, too."

Ruth wasn't accustomed to being around children. Hopefully, the boys wouldn't get on her nerves. They could be a bit rambunctious at times.

Gloria headed to the barn with her heavy-duty flashlight. She unlocked the door and pulled it to the side. She beamed the light in. The place was filling up fast! Ruth followed her out and the two women shuffled boxes to the side to make room for Jill's contribution.

They cleared a path and emptied a corner section. Ruth stood back and surveyed the piles. "What happens to the stuff we don't sell?"

Gloria crossed her arms. She hadn't put much thought into that part yet. "Call one of those donation centers to come pick it up?" She pushed the hair back from her eyes. The days were running together. "What day is today?"

"Thursday. Why?"

"We *could* start the sale Saturday, take a break on Sunday and then wrap it up with a bang on Monday!"

The more Gloria thought about it, the more she liked the idea. That way, it would keep Ruth busy, but it would also help them get rid of as much stuff as possible. It didn't make sense to Gloria to have a one-day sale. Not with all the stuff they had!

Ruth nodded. "We could organize tomorrow and start the sale Saturday."

Headlights flashed across the lawn and then beamed in through the barn doors. It was Jill.

Gloria's grandsons, Tyler and Ryan, bolted out of the back doors and ran to Gloria. She bent down and wrapped an arm around each of them. "Boy, have I missed you two!"

It had been a couple weeks since Gloria had stopped by Jill's place. "We need to plan a sleepover at Gram's house," she told them.

Ryan pulled back. He looked up at his beloved Grams. "Really??"

He turned to his mother. "Can we, Mom? Gram's asking..."

Jill shook her head. "You sure you're ready for that?"

The last time the boys had spent the weekend, they'd had loads of excitement. Between discovering someone hiding out in Gloria's barn, to the boys catching a snake, to finding a dead body in Andrea's shed. Yes, it had been an eventful weekend.

But what were the chances of having all that excitement happen again? She glanced at Ruth. The only problem was, she wasn't certain how much longer Ruth would be staying. And

Gloria didn't want her to feel like she was pushing her out....

Jill must've read Gloria's mind. She ruffled Ryan's hair. "We'll talk about it later."

The group had the trunk of Jill's car unloaded in record time. Most of what she had brought over was clothes. There was only a small box of toys. Gloria pointed at the small box. "Those are the only toys you have?"

Tyler eyed the box with suspicion. "Mom was trying to get rid of all our good toys!" he told his grandmother.

Gloria smiled at Tyler. "Why don't you boys run on ahead into the house and wash your hands?"

The boys raced off to the house and the girls trailed behind. "I figured I'd wait 'til the boys are playing over at their friend's house tomorrow and then I can clean out their rooms," Jill said.

"Good idea." Gloria nodded. "Ruth and I decided to have the sale Saturday *and* Monday. We figured it didn't make much sense to do all this work for just one day."

"I can come help both days," she offered. She grabbed the bags of burgers and fries from the front seat. "I'll have to bring the boys," she warned.

"Of course. We can put them in charge of crowd control," Gloria joked.

Tyler and Ryan were inside, chasing Mally in circles around the dining room table. The boys would suddenly stop and start running in the opposite direction and Mally would start chasing them.

Puddles, Gloria's cat, was nowhere in sight.

"Let's eat!" Jill hollered into the dining room. She turned to Gloria. "I hope burgers are okay."

Gloria nodded. "Sounds perfect. Thanks for bringing it."

Ruth reached for her purse. "Dinner's on me. How much do I owe you?" she asked.

Jill handed her a wrapped burger and packet of fries. "No, you don't have to do that Ruth."

Ruth took the food from Jill and set it down on the table. "I insist. It's the least I can do."

Jill told her the amount and Ruth handed her that, plus a little extra.

The group prayed over the food before digging in.

"Do you need me to come back tomorrow to help organize?" Jill dipped a fry in ketchup and took a bite.

"I think Ruth and I can handle it," Gloria said. "Just plan on coming early Saturday."

Tyler kicked his feet under his chair. "We can help, too, Grams."

Gloria smiled at her grandson. "Why, thank you Tyler. I'm sure you'll be a big help."

They finished the food, then Gloria collected the wrappers and dropped them inside the bags. She shoved the bags in the trash can and closed the lid.

Ruth picked up her phone. "I'll text the other girls and let them know we're starting the sale on Saturday."

Jill looked at her watch. "We better go. It's getting late. Greg will be home by now."

Gloria walked Jill and the boys to the car. Jill glanced back at the house. "How much longer will Ruth be staying?" she whispered.

Gloria followed her gaze. She shrugged her shoulders. "I don't know. Not too much longer, I hope."

Jill drove off, but not before she promised her mother she'd be back at 8:00 Saturday morning for the yard sale.

The girls were up bright and early the next morning, prepared to tackle the yard sale project. Lucy was the first to show up. She brought another small load of stuff with her. Margaret was next. She had a trunk full and promised that was the end.

Gloria eyed all the goodies Margaret pulled from her trunk. She made a mental note to take a good look at everything before the sale started. Just in case there was something she couldn't live without!

Dot was the last to arrive. She had the largest load. Gloria pulled a box from the back of the van. "I had no idea you even owned this much stuff," Gloria grumbled.

Dot reached in and grabbed a floor fan. "Yeah, me either."

Lucy wandered over to help. She pulled out a wooden end table then grabbed a used coffee maker. She sniffed the air. "Do I smell donuts?"

Dot reached into the passenger seat and pulled out a bakery box. "Leave it to Lucy to sniff out the sweets," she teased.

She handed the box to Ruth then grabbed a carafe of coffee and a pack of Styrofoam cups.

"Dot to the rescue," Margaret declared.

The girls circled several lawn chairs and sat down to take a break. Ruth pulled a glazed donut from the box before passing the box on to Lucy. Lucy picked a pink frosted donut with sprinkles and started to hand the box to Margaret. "I might as well take two now," she decided. She grabbed a raspberry twist before surrendering the box.

Gloria pulled a card table from the wall and set it up in the middle of the circle. She poured cups of coffee before the donut box reached her. At least they left her favorite. A chocolate éclair.

Lucy licked pink frosting from her upper lip. "I left that for you," she told Gloria.

Gloria set the frosted confection on a napkin and reached for her coffee. "Thanks, Lucy." They each had a different favorite and after all these years, Dot knew who liked what and made sure to bring at least one of each.

Margaret broke off a piece of her apple turnover. "How's the investigation at the post office going?"

They all turned to Ruth. Her face fell. She set her donut on the napkin. "I wish I knew."

Dot poured a liquid creamer in her coffee and stirred. "I'd march right over there and demand an update," she said. "You have a right to know."

The group agreed that Ruth should stop by there to check in.

Gloria sipped her coffee. "That might not be a bad idea, Ruth. After all, I think it would look suspicious if you didn't..."

Ruth turned to Gloria. "You really think so?"

A murmured agreement by all was enough to convince Ruth to stop by there later. She popped last piece of donut in her mouth, a look of determination on her face. "You're right. You're all right!"

The group finished the breakfast and dumped the trash in a bin Gloria had dragged out for the sale.

Earlier, Gloria had assembled a makeshift rack to hang the clothes on. It ran the entire length of the barn wall.

The toys were put in one group, while dishes and other miscellaneous household items were put in another. Gloria began to pull the items from the boxes and set them on the long rows of card tables. There were lamps, clocks, place mats. And then Gloria ran across an odd looking item. It was round and it looked like a black ball. A small instruction sheet was taped to the bottom. She held it up. "What's this?"

Ruth was stacking books on a table nearby. "Is this yours?" Gloria asked.

Ruth looked at the round object. "Yeah." She glanced around to see if anyone was listening in.

Gloria leaned closer. "Is that what I think it is?"

Ruth nodded. "Yep. It's a mini camera. I had this one over at the post office 'til I upgraded to the one I have there now." She gave Gloria a hard look.

Gloria turned it over in her hand. "Does it work?"

"Like a charm," Ruth said. "Only problem was, it was a little small and had limited scope. You know, I couldn't see as much as I can with the upgraded model. Super easy to use, too. You can use it with your phone to spy on people!"

Gloria nodded. She pretended to set it back down. When Ruth turned away, she stuck it in the pocket of her sweater. Somehow, she had a feeling it might come in handy.

The five of them worked right along and a couple hours later everything was organized and ready to go.

Dot was the first to leave. "I'd offer to help tomorrow..."

Gloria nodded. "I appreciate that Dot, but I know you have the restaurant to run." She went on. "Ruth will be here and so will Jill."

Lucy and Margaret had more flexibility and told Gloria they'd be there around 9:00. Then Gloria remembered Andrea.

Andrea had asked if she could take a look at everything before it went up for sale. Gloria pulled the phone from her pocket and texted her.

Lucy was the last to leave. She put a hand on Ruth's shoulder. "I can go to the post office with you," she said, "for moral support."

Ruth took a deep breath and straightened her shoulders. "Thanks, Lucy, but I need to take care of this on my own."

Lucy drove off while Andrea pulled in. "This place is like a revolving door," Ruth observed.

Andrea parked in front of the barn doors. She slid out of her sports car and held the door open. Brutus bounded out and over to Gloria.

Mally had been wandering around inside the barn sniffing everything. When she saw Brutus, she did an about-face and came close to check out the visitor.

Andrea grabbed hold of Brutus's collar. "Sit," she commanded. Brutus obeyed Andrea and sat.

Gloria reached for Mally's collar. "Mally sit, too." Mally sat. Her eyes never left Brutus. Then Mally thumped her tail. Just a bit.

Brutus thumped his tail in response.

"I think that's a good sign." Gloria bent down. "Mally, this is Brutus. Brutus, Mally."

The two dogs sniffed the air. Then Mally crouched down and pulled herself forward with her front paws. She looked at Brutus, then looked away. Brutus thumped his tail again.

Mally pulled herself closer. At the same time, both dogs leaned forward to sniff each other, then barked "hello" at the same time.

"Well, I'll be." Andrea shook her head. "They like each other."

Gloria released her hold on Mally's collar first. Andrea let go of Brutus's collar. Brutus sniffed while Mally pranced. When Mally tried to lead Brutus out of the barn, Gloria stopped her. "Whoa! I don't think you two should wander off."

She looked up at Andrea. "I'll be right back." She led Mally back to the house and put her indoors. She was glad the two got along but wasn't sure if Mally wouldn't be so excited to show Brutus around that they might run off down the road. To the neighbor's chicken coop or somewhere else they shouldn't be.

By the time she headed back to the barn, Andrea had grabbed a set of delicate china and placed it on the front seat of her car. "I think those are Dot's," Ruth observed.

Gloria pulled the colored tag from the top plate. "Yep."

Andrea picked out a few more things before announcing she was done. She handed Gloria a hundred dollar bill. Gloria looked at the money. "I'm sure the stuff wasn't that much."

Andrea grinned. "This will help jump start your sales." She hugged Gloria good-bye and climbed into her car.

Gloria closed the barn door and put the padlock in place. "I think I'll head to the post office before I chicken out," Ruth decided. She grabbed her purse and car keys then headed to the van. Gloria waited until her van was out of sight before she headed to the spare bedroom. The bedroom Ruth was staying in.

She pushed the door open and peeked her head around the corner. The room was tidy. The bed was made and the curtains open wide to let sunshine in.

Gloria stepped all the way inside and over to the dresser. She sucked in a breath when she saw a white box on the floor next to the dresser. It looked like the box that Kenny had handed her at his house the other morning.

Gloria lifted the box and set it on top of the dresser. She folded the cardboard top back and looked inside. It contained a single item - a plastic box. It looked like a fishing tackle box. She lifted it out and held it up to the light from the window.

Inside the box she could see small divided compartments or bins but she couldn't make out what was in them. The frosted cover blocked the view. She turned it around and her heart plummeted. There was a small combination lock on the front!

She pulled the box close to her face and sniffed the lid. There was no odor.   She shook it gently. There was no noise. Frustrated, she dropped the box inside the cardboard container, closed the lid and set it back on the floor.

Whatever was in the box was something Ruth didn't want others seeing. Why else would it be locked?

Gloria remembered the mini spy camera. She pulled it out of her pocket and peeled the instruction sheet off the back. She went into the kitchen and grabbed her glasses from the table. The instructions *looked* fairly simple. She switched the button to "on" then headed back to Ruth's room.

She needed to put it in a spot where it wasn't sticking out like a sore thumb. The perfect spot was a small shelf loaded with collectibles Gloria had accumulated over the years. She tucked the black ball between two of the darker objects and stood back. She could barely see it. Unless Ruth was looking for it, she'd never even notice!

She grabbed her phone and scrolled through her apps screen. What was the name of that thing? She remembered seeing it stamped on the side. Was the name of it - *My Spy*? She scrolled some more. There it was! *Eye Spy!* She clicked on the name and waited while it loaded. The screen changed and suddenly she was staring inside the bedroom and right at the dresser where Ruth normally kept her purse. She could even see the floor where the box sat.

She switched the phone off and took it to her bedroom where she set it on the dresser. Gloria closed her bedroom door and wandered back into the kitchen just in time to see Ruth come up the steps. She opened the door and waited for her to step in. "How'd it go?"

She could tell by the look on Ruth's face it wasn't good. "They said they were hours away from wrapping up the investigation and making an arrest."

"Well, that's good! Then you can get back to work," Gloria said.

Ruth shook her head and frowned. "I don't think so. By the tone of Sharon's voice, I think they plan to arrest me!"

Gloria's mouth fell open as Ruth pulled out a chair and slumped down. "Something about how they have more than enough evidence now."

"But why you?"

Ruth dropped her chin in her fist. "Maybe because they really don't have a suspect and I'm as good a scapegoat as any?" She shrugged her shoulders and tears filled her eyes. "I've never been to jail before."

Gloria remembered the mountain trip when she, Liz and Margaret had ended up in jail overnight. She shuddered at the thought.

She patted Ruth's arm. "The Lord won't let that happen."

She grabbed her Bible off the side shelf and flipped it open to one of her favorite verses.

Psalm 143:1 (NIV)

Lord, hear my prayer, listen to my cry for mercy; in your faithfulness and righteousness come to my relief.

The women bowed their heads and prayed that Ruth would not be wrongly accused and that the true criminal would be brought to justice and their actions brought to light.

Ruth wiped the tears and gave Gloria a watery smile. "Thanks for being such a great friend."

"We're going to get to the bottom of this," Gloria vowed. "Soon."

Ruth didn't pull her laptop back out. She didn't seem interested anymore in the goings on at the post office. Instead, she plopped down on the living room sofa and stared at the TV the rest of the afternoon. Gloria knew she wasn't watching it. She didn't bother to pick up the remote, which was right next to her. She never turned the channel. Not once.

When dinnertime came, Gloria asked if she wanted grilled cheese and soup. She stared blankly at Gloria, then shook her head "no."

But Gloria made her one despite her objections. She wandered into the living room with both their plates and set Ruth's on her lap. "You have to eat something."

Instead of argue, Ruth lifted the sandwich and took a small bite. When the sandwich was gone, Gloria took her plate and returned with a piping hot mug of tomato soup and pile of crackers. "Here, eat this."

Ruth crumbled a few crackers into the soup and spooned the mixture into her mouth. The glazed expression never left her face.

When they finished, Gloria washed up the few dishes and returned to the living room to find Ruth in the same position she'd left her in. For once, Gloria didn't know how to help. She didn't know how to fix this for Ruth.

Gloria was sinking as far down-in-the-dumps as Ruth herself was.

She let Mally out one last time and decided to head to bed. Tomorrow was going to be a busy day for the girls. Hopefully, it was one that wouldn't include Ruth's arrest!

Chapter 7

Cars were lined up in the driveway and on the road in front of the house by 7:00 a.m. Saturday morning. News of the yard sale traveled far and wide. The fact that several families would be involved and the sale would have lots of antiques and children's clothes brought them in droves. It didn't hurt that Dot told every person that came into the restaurant that they were having a sale at Gloria's.

By the time Margaret and Lucy showed up at 8:15, the place was jam-packed. Gloria put Tyler and Ryan in charge of keeping an eye on the kids in the crowd, who tended to wander off when their parents weren't looking, and the first place they headed was in the direction of the busy road!

As soon as Lucy arrived, Gloria pulled her aside. "I need your help inside."

Lucy raised her eyebrows but obediently followed Gloria across the drive and into the house.

Gloria pulled her phone from her pocket and turned it on. They were the only two in the house. "I set up a small surveillance camera in Ruth's bedroom. I need you to stay inside and keep an eye on it. I have a hunch something's going to happen today."

Lucy nodded. "Okay. I'm certainly not one to question your hunches."

"There's only one thing," Gloria went on. "You need to stay out of sight. You know, so no one knows you're in here."

She grabbed Lucy's arm and pulled her to her bedroom. "You can hang out in here."

After she settled Lucy in the room and showed her how the camera worked, she headed back outside.

Thank goodness no one seemed to notice Lucy was MIA. They were all too busy helping customers with their purchases. Gloria recognized a lot of the faces in the crowd. But there were quite a few she didn't recognize.

Dot dropped by at noon. There was a small lull in the crowds. She brought a tray of sandwiches and salads. Gloria headed indoors to grab Lucy, hoping no one would notice she hadn't been around.

She ducked her head around the bedroom door to find Lucy reclining on her bed. "See anything yet?"

Lucy sprang up. She shook her head. "Nope. Not a thing."

Gloria stuck her hand on her hip. "I hope my hunch wasn't wrong."

They wandered out to the others and gathered around an empty card table. The tables were clearing out fast.

Dot glanced around. "Wow, a lot of stuff is already gone! Any idea how much money we've made?"

Ruth was in charge of sales. She stuck her hand in the metal box they were using as a cash register. She pulled out a wad of bills. "I haven't had a chance to count, but look at all of this!"

The group had decided at the last minute, for the sake of convenience, to split the money evenly. They decided that, other than Dot, they'd all contributed about the same amount of stuff. Dot didn't seem to mind. She was just happy to have her house cleaned out.

They finished their food and got back to work. Lucy gave Gloria a dark look and headed back inside to finish her stakeout. Gloria was itching to do it herself but knew that if she stayed inside someone would notice.

Gloria's heart sank when she saw Sharon McIntyre, the post office detective, pull into the drive. Ruth had also noticed her pull up. The color drained from her face and she clutched at her throat.

Gloria met her at her car. "This is a surprise, Detective McIntyre." The woman reminded Gloria of a younger version of Joyce Jameson, the female detective on her favorite series, *Detective on the Side*. She was tall and thin. Her shoulder length blonde hair was parted off to one side. She wore little makeup and every time Gloria saw her, she had the same frown on her face, as if she hated her job and made sure everyone knew it.

The woman straightened her frame and peered down at Gloria. "This isn't a social call, Mrs. Rutherford," she said. "I'm here to see Ruth Carpenter."

Several of the customers stopped to stare. Margaret came to stand near Ruth. She put a protective hand on her shoulder.

The detective spied Ruth and walked over to her. She bent forward and began to talk in a low voice. "I need to bring you down to the post office to meet with one of the other of the detectives."

Ruth gulped. "Right now?"

The woman nodded and looked at the gathering crowd. "Yes, now."

Gloria stepped in. "Surely you can see that we need Ruth. We can come down in a few hours when we close the sale," she bargained.

But Detective McIntyre was having none of that. She shook her head.

Ruth reluctantly stood and shuffled along behind the detective as she headed to the unmarked police car.

Gloria was torn. She wanted to go. To support Ruth, but she couldn't leave now! The timing couldn't have been worse! She stomped her foot. That stupid detective knew exactly what she was doing!

Maybe Andrea could run up there and show a little moral support. Or even Dot! She turned on her heel and headed towards the house. She was halfway across the drive when Lucy ran out the front door. She waved frantically at Gloria.

"You're never gonna believe..." Gloria said.

Lucy cut her off. "No! You're never gonna believe what I just saw!" She tapped the front of the phone. Then she looked over Gloria's head and made a weird statement. "Good. She's gone!"

Gloria was confused. "You're *glad* they took Ruth away?" She must've heard Lucy wrong!

"Huh?" Now it was Lucy's turn to be confused. She waved her inside.

She pulled out a kitchen chair for Gloria. "Grab your glasses and have a seat!"

Gloria pulled her reading glasses from the center of the table and slipped them on.

Lucy pulled out the chair next to her and dropped down. "I was bored earlier so I started playing with this camera-thingy and I figured out how to record stuff."

"That's good." So that was what Lucy was excited about?

"Right after I figured out how to do that, you'll never guess what happened!" Lucy shoved the phone into Gloria's hand and pushed a button on the screen.

Gloria watched in silence as a figure crept into Ruth's room. At first, Gloria couldn't make out of a face. Only that it was the more petite figure of a female. The person tip-toed over to Ruth's purse and opened it up, then slipped something inside before turning back around. When the figure turned around, the camera got a clear shot of the face.

Gloria's hand flew to her mouth. "You know who that is!"

Lucy nodded. "After she left, I went right into Ruth's room and opened her purse."

Gloria's head shot up. She stared into Lucy's eyes. "What was it?"

Lucy sprang from the chair. "C'mon. I'll show you!"

Gloria followed Lucy into Ruth's room and over to the chair. The purse was still there and it was open. She leaned over and looked inside. She lifted her eyes and stared at Lucy. "Is this what I think it is?"

"It has to be cocaine. I mean, I've only seen it on TV but that's what it looks like to me," she theorized.

Gloria stood straight up. "We need to get down to the post office right away," she said. "Maybe they haven't arrested Ruth yet."

It was Lucy's turn. "Arrested Ruth? Why Ruth's still outside..."

Gloria shook her head. "Detective McIntyre just took her away in her car." She looked down at the purse. "Don't touch that. It's evidence." She hugged Lucy. "Thank you, Lord, that you showed Lucy how to record on that crazy phone."

Gloria looked around the room. Propped up in the corner was a wooden dowel she used to hold the bedroom window open in the summer months. She plucked it out of the corner and used the end to lift the purse up. She carried it outside.

Jill and Margaret were huddled together near the money table. Margaret's eyes were red and puffy. She wiped at a tear with the back of her hand. "I can't believe they took Ruth away!"

"Not for long," Gloria insisted. "Not after they see the evidence Lucy and I have."

Lucy stepped around the side of Gloria. "We have to get down to the post office right away."

Tyler wandered over to the table. "We can take care of things here, Grams."

She smiled down at Tyler. Well, not really smiled *down*. He was getting tall now, almost as tall as Gloria herself. "Thank you, Tyler."

There was no time to lose. "We'll be back in a jiffy."

Gloria climbed into Lucy's jeep. They started to back out when a vehicle pulled in behind them, blocking their path. Gloria glanced in the rearview mirror. Judging by the outfit the man had on, it was another detective. He was wearing a pair of dark sunglasses and his expression was grim.

He walked right by the jeep and headed to the porch door. Gloria climbed back out of the jeep and followed him up the steps. "Can I help you?"

The man turned around. "I'm looking for Gloria Rutherford," he said.

"That would be me," she answered.

"I'm here to pick up Ruth Carpenter's purse."

Gloria pointed to Lucy's jeep. It's in the jeep. We were headed to the post office with it when you pulled in behind us and blocked our vehicle."

The stone-faced man looked at the jeep. "I'll take it." He didn't wait for an answer as he side-stepped Gloria and headed to the vehicle. He walked straight over to the passenger side, reached inside and grabbed the purse.

Gloria furrowed her brows. *Great detective he is, contaminating evidence with his prints!* she thought.

Without uttering a single word, he walked back to this car, climbed inside and backed out of the driveway.

"What was that all about?" Lucy wondered.

Gloria shook her head in disgust. "Terrible detective work, that's what."

They turned the jeep around and headed to town. Gloria prayed for Ruth on the way, that they hadn't taken her to jail yet.

Gloria's stomach twisted in a tight knot when they pulled up in front of the post office and saw half a dozen unmarked vehicles parked out front. The girls could see straight inside the large plate glass window.

Ruth was in view, her back to them as several people stood around her in a small circle. Gloria stepped forward and tapped on the glass window. One of the men in the group looked up at them then shook his head.

But Gloria was NOT about to give up. They had evidence and these detectives needed to see it! She tapped again, but this time harder.

They all looked up now. One of them signaled Gloria and Lucy around to the rear. A man was outside waiting for them. "The post office isn't open," he said as they approached.

Lucy rolled her eyes. "We *know* that! We have evidence in this case."

"What kind of evidence?" he asked.

Gloria switched the "on" button on her phone and hit the play button for the recording Lucy had made a short time ago. "This! Ruth Carpenter is being framed!"

The man watched the video in silence. "Where did you get this?" he asked after the video ended.

"A small spy camera was installed in the corner of the room where Ruth's purse was. The video recorded this woman planting drugs in her purse."

He nodded. "That package of cocaine was found in her bag."

"Who's the woman in the video?" he asked.

Instead of answer his question, Gloria pushed aside and opened the screen door. "Sharon McIntyre knows exactly who this is. Let's ask her!"

She barged into the rear of the post office. All the heads swung around as they heard the commotion. Gloria and Ruth's eyes met. Gloria's heart sank when she saw her friend's swollen, red face.

She walked up to Detective McIntyre and thrust the phone into her hand. "Watch this video," she said.

The group of detectives clustered around the small screen and watched the video. The only one who couldn't see it was Ruth. "Ruth's been set up," she said.

Sharon shook her head in disbelief. "Where did you get this?"

Once again, Gloria explained how she had set up the camera in Ruth's room and Lucy had monitored it during the sale on a hunch that something was going to happen.

"Well, this changes everything," Sharon McIntyre announced.

Lucy took a step closer. "That means that Ruth is free to go?"

Sharon slowly nodded. "Turns out my informant is the real culprit."

Ruth abruptly burst into tears when it sank in she was free to go. That she was no longer a suspect and that she wasn't going to be arrested. She flung her arms around Gloria's neck and sobbed. Gloria held her friend in a tight grip. Lucy circled the two and all three of them hugged for a long moment.

When they took a step back, the detective stepped forward. She touched Ruth's arm. "I'm sorry for the grief and aggravation we've caused you these last few days but I might have to ask for your help."

Ruth sniffled and eyed the detective warily.

She went on. "We'd like to set up a sting. You know, catch the true criminal in the act and I think you can be of assistance."

Gloria's heart skipped a beat. That would be right up her alley. Maybe she could play a small part!

Ruth grabbed Gloria's hand in a death grip. "Only if Gloria can be a part of it," she bargained.

Sharon gazed at Gloria. "I suppose." She turned back to Ruth. "We'll need to set a trap of sorts. Something to draw her. Catch her in the act, so to speak."

She tapped the side of her head. "The only thing is, I want to catch her red-handed and she thinks you're on your way to jail."

Gloria's mind was spinning. "What if you tell her that you're trying to catch RUTH in the act? That will force her to act rashly ... to try to plant more drugs."

She went on. "We make it convenient for her to do that. All the while, someone is watching with a camera and Voila! Busted."

Sharon nodded. "That might work. We tell Tammy Dillon that we're keeping her at this post office to keep an eye on Ruth. You know, to try and catch her in the act."

Ruth's face got red. "I have a better idea." Ruth made a squeezing motion with her hands. "I'll just wrap my hands around her chicken neck and strangle her to death!"

Lucy patted her arm. "Now, Ruth. You have to play it cool. Like you have no idea that she framed you and tried to send you up river!"

Gloria cleared her throat. "Ahem."

Lucy shrugged. "Well, she did."

Ruth dropped her hands to her side. "I can do it. I know I can," she vowed.

The other detectives headed out the door. Sharon was the last to leave. "I'll have Tammy here Monday morning at 8 sharp for work."

She gave Ruth a hard look. "Are you sure you can do this?"

Ruth nodded firmly. "Yes. One hundred percent." She pounded her fist on her palm. "We're gonna take her down!"

Chapter 8

Ruth was up early for church the next morning. The bounce was back in her step, a light in her eyes. Gloria was up early, too. She was thrilled for Ruth but more than that, Gloria loved Sundays. It was her day to be in the Lord's house and no matter how rough her week had been, she was filled with God's presence and peace on Sunday.

Gloria poured a cup of coffee and sat in the seat next to Ruth, who had just opened the Sunday paper.

Ruth lifted her head and studied Gloria's face. "That was my little spy camera you used to catch Tammy," she said.

Gloria grinned and nodded. "Yeah. Sure came in handy."

Ruth folded the paper up and set it to the side. "How did you know to do that?"

Gloria eyed her friend. She shrugged and reached for an apple from the basket of fruit in the center of the table. "Just a hunch."

"Did you think it was me?" Ruth asked.

Gloria shook her head. The truth was, in her heart, she knew it could never be Ruth. Not after knowing her friend all these years...

"No." But Gloria did have a question. "I did wonder what was in the tackle box, though," she admitted.

Ruth didn't answer. She jumped out of the chair and headed to the bedroom. She came back with the tackle box in hand. The lid was unlatched. She set it on the table and pushed it over to Gloria. "Go ahead. Look inside."

Gloria lifted the lid. The box was full of stamps. She picked a pile up and sifted through them. Each was unique. Many of them looked old. "I had to send Kenny into the post office one night to get these for me," Ruth explained.

"I kept them in a locked drawer. It's a collection I started years ago when I first started working at the post office." Ruth picked one up and studied the front. "It was a hobby at first but now I think some of them are valuable." She dropped the stamp back on top. "I thought if the detectives found these, they'd think that I stole them."

Gloria nodded. That would explain why she saw Kenny staring into the camera that night he was in the post office. Ruth had sent him on a mission to retrieve the stamp collection.

That must have been what Ruth picked up at Kenny's that morning at his house.

Still, if it was an inside job, was Kenny in on it with Tammy? she wondered. She didn't dare tell Ruth she'd followed her to Kenny's the other morning.

She looked at the clock. It was time to go. "I'm ready to move back home," Ruth announced.

Gloria glanced at her. "Okay," she said.

Ruth went on. "Right after church I'll grab my things. That way I can spend the afternoon getting the house in order to be back at work in the morning."

Ruth scraped the chair across the linoleum floor and stood. "Detective Sharon told me she'd stop by later today to go over our sting operation."

Gloria felt a twinge of envy. She wished *she* was in on the sting operation. But maybe it was best that she wasn't. Tammy was Ruth's nemesis – not hers.

The church was packed. She and Ruth wandered in just before the choir started to sing. Lucy and Margaret had saved them a spot and the girls squeezed in beside them with Ruth on the end of the pew.

Margaret leaned forward. "I heard that you're going back to work tomorrow," she said.

Ruth nodded and Margaret gave her the thumbs up. The congregation stood for the singing and that was the end of the talk.

Pastor Nate's message was thought-provoking. It was about angels in disguise and how when we help others less fortunate we may be helping angels in disguise. The key verse was:

"Be not forgetful to entertain strangers: for thereby some have entertained angels unawares. Hebrews 13:2 KJV

The service ended and the girls met outside in their usual spot underneath the big oak tree, at the edge of the parking lot. "Any new shut-ins this week we need to visit?" Gloria asked. There hadn't been too many lately. Everyone seemed to be out and about with the nice weather.

Margaret hesitated. "There is one." Everyone looked at her. "It's Judith Arnett. She twisted her back swatting at some squirrels that were digging holes around her rose bushes."

Dot looked away. Lucy cleared her throat. Ruth spoke up. "I'd go but I have to get back home and do some work around the house to get ready for work tomorrow," she explained.

"I'll go visit her," Gloria announced. All heads spun around and stared at Gloria. She took a deep breath. It would be hard to explain how she'd had a change of heart about Judith after Judith tried to help Ruth. Even though Judith was still a petty thief and gossiper, she could change. Plus, it wasn't her place to judge. "I have some extras from the garden to take her and now that Ruth's moving out, I don't have plans for the afternoon."

The excuse did sound a little lame but she had another reason to visit Judith. To see if she'd stumbled upon anything else by chance. They had Tammy, for sure. But what about the fact that everyone seemed to think someone on the inside was involved...

Back at the farm, Ruth packed up and headed out. She didn't even hang around to have lunch with Gloria before she left. Gloria rattled around the empty house for a few minutes before she noticed the light on her answering machine was blinking. She pressed the button.

"Hi Grams." She recognized Tyler's voice. "Ryan and I were wondering if we could come and spend the night at your house tonight." He lowered his voice. "We didn't ask Mom yet 'cuz we know she'd tell us no." He sounded so grown up. "Call me back." The call ended abruptly.

Gloria erased the message. The house *was* lonely. The boys would liven it up, for sure. Plus, they would be here the next morning for the final day of the yard sale, anyways. She picked up the phone and dialed her daughter's number. "Hello?"

"Hi, Jill. It's Mom. Ruth went home and the house seems a bit empty today. Do you mind if the boys come spend the night with me?"

Jill paused. "Are you sure you're up for that? I mean, the boys would be thrilled."

The more Gloria thought about it, the more she liked the idea. "I could put them to work organizing the rest of the yard sale stuff for me," she said.

"Okay. If you're sure...."

Gloria could hear whoops of joy in the background as the boys overheard the conversation. They were going to Gram's farm!

She remembered her promise to visit Judith. "I have a couple errands to run but the boys can go with me."

"If you're positive they won't be too much trouble..." Jill's voice trailed off.

"Yes, I'm sure. You can bring them by any time," she said.

Ryan must've taken the phone from his mother. "We're on our way, Grams!" The line disconnected. Gloria grinned. She looked down at Mally. "The boys are coming for a visit!"

Gloria pulled a package of hot dogs from the freezer to unthaw for dinner. They could work on the barn, then grill the hotdogs and some corn on the cob for dinner. But first, they needed to get over to Judith's place.

Jill's car made the trip in record time. Gloria was certain the boys had driven her nuts until she relented and headed over. The car wasn't even shut off before the boys darted out the doors and raced to the porch. Tyler reached her first. He wrapped his arms around her waist and hugged her as if he hadn't seen her for days. Although both had been there the day before for the sale. She hugged them both, then looked at her daughter. Jill's face was filled with concern. "Are you *sure* you're up for this?"

"Absolutely." She released her grip on the boys as Jill handed them their backpacks and they headed inside. "Don't worry, they'll be helping me, too."

Gloria hugged her daughter. "Go. Have a nice dinner with Greg. Enjoy the evening off."

Jill smiled. "Thanks, Mom. I love you."

For some reason, the words choked Gloria up and tears filled her eyes. Gloria's family was precious to her. She never wanted to take them for granted or have them feel they weren't important to her.

She watched as Jill backed out of the drive, then she headed inside. The boys had raided the cookie jar and helped themselves to some chocolate chip cookies Gloria had made the other day. Before all heck broke loose with Ruth.

She poured each a glass of milk and joined them at the table.

"We have to stop by my friend Judith's place for a few minutes before we come back and clean up the barn," she explained.

A thought popped into her head. "You two are my big helpers today and I'm going to pay each of you ten dollars after we're done working." Gloria wasn't sure if the boys earned an allowance. If not, it was time for them to learn the value of earning a dollar. She wasn't even sure if ten dollars was the going rate, but judging by the expression on their face, it was good pay.

The boys turned to each other. *"Ten dollars?"* They quickly finished their snack and headed to the car.

Judith's small ranch home was on the other side of town. She'd remembered to call ahead and make sure Judith would be home. She had also warned her the boys would be tagging along. Judith's voice sounded a little strained, as if she was in pain, but she seemed glad for the company. "Just let yourselves in when you get here," she said. "I'm having a hard time getting off the couch."

When Gloria heard that, she decided to throw the extra batch of spaghetti pie she'd made the other night in the bag, along with the vegetables.

They pulled into Judith's drive, right behind her car. They let themselves in the side door and into the kitchen. Gloria set the food on the counter.

"In here," a weak voice called from the other room. Gloria had never been inside Judith's house before. It was neat and tidy and smelled like Pine Sol. Judith was sprawled out on the couch, flat on her back. Her face was pale.

Gloria walked over to the sofa and looked down. "Oh, Judith. You look like you're in a lot of pain," she said.

Ryan tugged on Gloria's hand. "Can we go outside Grams?"

Gloria nodded. "Stay in the yard. And stay away from the rose bushes," she added.

They darted out the door. Gloria could hear them clamber down the steps. She made her way over to the recliner and eased onto the edge. "I brought a spaghetti pie for dinner and some vegetables from the garden," Gloria said. "Is there anything else I can do?"

Judith shook her head. "No. I took a pain pill but that only took the edge off." She let out a big sigh. "Thanks for the food. Carl will be happy." Carl was Judith's husband.

A movement past the front picture window caught her eye. She caught a glimpse of the boys' heads as they ran past the window.

"Did you hear Ruth is going back to work in the morning?"

Judith's eyes flew open. She turned her head towards Gloria. "Really? Thank the Lord. The woman that was running the place was incompetent!"

"You didn't happen to get a chance to – you know – keep an eye on the post office again..."

Judith dropped a dramatic hand to her side. "Funny you should mention that. As a matter of fact, I did. Right before I hurt my back. I saw a woman and someone that looked like Kenny out behind the post office the other night."

Ruth went on. "Of course, it was dark so I wasn't 100% certain." She waved her hand to the coffee table. "I got a picture but it's dark and grainy. Maybe you can make more out of it than I could."

Gloria picked up the phone on the table and switched it to on. She could make out Tammy as the petite figure. The other figure was shorter. Gloria tapped the screen and zoomed in.

It looked familiar but Gloria wasn't 100% convinced it was Kenny. She looked up at Judith. "Can I send this picture to my phone?"

Judith nodded. "Sure."

Gloria forwarded the picture and set the phone back on the coffee table.

"Grams! Come quick!" It was Ryan. Gloria jumped to her feet and ran to the door. He waved her to the side, then disappeared from sight. She took the steps two at a time in hot pursuit. She rounded the corner of the house and spotted the boys. They were bent over what looked to be some sort of cage. Ryan pointed inside. "Look what we caught!"

Gloria peeked around the side of him and into the cage that Tyler was standing next to. Inside the cage was a large, red squirrel. He hovered in the corner, his beady eyes stared up at them. "How did you catch him?" Without getting bit – or scratched – she said to herself.

Tyler shrugged. "It was easy. Ryan ran after him while I held the cage. He ran inside and I shut the door."

Gloria raised her eyebrows in disbelief. "Really? He just ran into the cage." She snapped her fingers. "Just like that!"

She didn't press the boys. The fact that they weren't harmed was reason enough to be thankful. "C'mon. Let's go tell Judith you got her pesky squirrel."

The boys raced her inside. By the time she got there, the boys had told her the story. She looked up at Gloria. "They really did get the squirrel?"

Gloria nodded. "Yep. It's in the cage out back."

"Can you grab my purse? It's over there on the bookcase," Judith said.

Gloria picked up her purse and brought it over to the couch. It took her a few minutes of fumbling around, but Judith finally managed to open her wallet and pull out two $5 bills. She handed one to each of the boys. "This is for you. Thank you for catching the squirrel for me."

The boys stared at the money in their outstretched hands. "Wow!" They looked at each. "Thank you." Tyler spoke first. "Yeah, thanks Mrs....." He looked at Gloria. "Mrs. Arnett," she told them.

"Thank you, Mrs. Arnett," they said in unison.

The trio made their way back outside and down the steps. The boys crawled into the back seat while Gloria climbed behind the wheel.

She smiled as she listened to the conversation in the back seat. "What are you going to do with your money?" Tyler asked his younger brother.

"I'm going to buy me that new race car game for Xbox," Ryan told him.

"You need a steering wheel to play it," Tyler pointed out.

"When Grams pays us for cleaning the barn, I'll have money for the steering wheel AND the game," Ryan answered.

Tyler shook his head. "Uh-uh. I think you need like $25 dollars for that."

Gloria glanced in the mirror. Ryan's mouth drooped and he dropped his chin. He stared down at the $5 bill clenched in his fist.

"If you do an *extra* good job, I'll give you each $20 instead of $10," she promised.

That perked Ryan right up. He was so excited, he started to kick the back of the driver's seat. "Really Grams? I'll do the best job ever," he promised.

Gloria's heart smiled. She made a vow to spend more time with the boys. They were growing up way too fast. It wouldn't be long and they would be too grown-up to want to spend time with her on the farm. She hoped that wouldn't happen, but kids these days got involved in all kinds of school activities and family tended to get pushed to the side.

The three of them changed into work clothes and then the trio and Mally headed to the barn. Gloria opened the lock and reached over to push the door open. Tyler stuck out his arm and stopped her. "No Grams. Let me do it this time."

Gloria stepped aside and watched with pride as her oldest grandson pushed both doors open. She blinked back tears once again. It reminded her of her husband, James, and how he loved the old barn. Tyler looked a lot like his grandfather and it melted her heart.

Gloria glanced around the barn in dismay. There was still quite a bit of stuff. The place was in shambles. The boys would be earning their $20!

She put Tyler in charge of hanging the tall heap of clothes that the customers had removed from the hangars and dropped in a pile on a table nearby.

She gave Ryan the task of picking up the toys. He darted back and forth across the barn floor as he picked up dolls, toy trains and a variety of other items that littered every corner of the barn. Gloria worked on consolidating some of the household stuff. She folded some of the tables and set them off to the side.

Mally was so excited to see the boys, she kept knocking knick knacks off the table and onto the floor with her happy tail. With the patience of a saint, Ryan would trudge over, pick the item up and set it back on the table.

When they were done, Gloria let Tyler shut the barn door. Ryan put the padlock on and snapped it shut.

Tyler looked at the Massey Ferguson tractor Gloria had pulled out of the barn. She had parked it off to the side so she could fit the yard sale stuff indoors. "Hey Grams, can you teach me how to drive that?" He pointed at the tractor.

Ryan hopped up and down on one foot. "Yeah! Me too, Grams. Can you teach me how to drive it, too?"

Gloria grinned. "Do you remember when Grandpa Rutherford used to take you boys around the fields in the tractor?"

"Uh-uh." They shook their heads in unison.

James loved to take the boys for rides. He'd tell Gloria that someday all of this would belong to them. She knew he always hoped the boys would love the farm as much as he had. She was sure James's face was beaming bright from heaven when he heard his grandsons beg to drive the tractor.

She put an arm around each of their shoulders as they walked back to the house. "Tell you what – as soon as the crops are out this fall,

I'll teach both of you how to drive the tractor," she promised.

She went on. "Now, how about some hotdogs for dinner?"

Ryan jumped up and down and spun around. "Yum-yum!" He rubbed his tummy. "I'm starving!"

She nodded to the garden. "Could you please go grab a few ears of corn?"

The boys left her in the dust as they raced each other to the rows of corn. She had a great thought as she watched them pluck corn from the stalks. She tiptoed across the plants. The boys each had an armful. Too many for dinner. She had showed them last year how to pull the husks back and check to see if they were ready to eat.

"You both earned your $20 in the barn," she said. "Would you like to earn a little more tomorrow?"

They both nodded eagerly.

"I need help in the garden. Someone to pick the ripe fruits and vegetables before they go bad." She went on. "Would you like to help me in the garden for another $10 each?

That was a bargain for Gloria! "We can start now," Ryan announced.

But Gloria shook her head. "No, it's time for dinner. You'll have plenty of time tomorrow," she assured them.

She shook her head as they headed indoors with Mally and the corn. She wished she had a third of the energy of just one of her grandsons. The work she could get done!

Dinner was a quick event and the boys were content to watch TV while Gloria checked her email and the weather forecast for the final day of the sale.

The boys didn't argue when it was time for bed. Mally settled in on the rug in front of them and listened as they said their bedtime prayers.

Gloria kissed them both. She thanked the Lord for her precious grandsons as she turned off the light and pulled the door shut.

Chapter 9

Ruth was up early the next morning. Early, as in before dawn. She had hardly slept a wink the night before. She was so excited about going back to work! To the place she loved! She vowed to never, ever grumble or complain about her job again!

Sharon had stopped by the night before. The two of them discussed a plan to catch Tammy Dillon red-handed, trying to frame Ruth. Ruth couldn't believe the woman – someone she considered a friend – to do something like that to her!

Ruth steeled herself to the task before her. After today, Ruth could put this whole thing behind her. Her name would be cleared and justice would be served. Thanks to Gloria! She owed her dear friend a great deal.

Ruth stuck her key in lock on the back door of the post office and swung it open. She flipped on the light and stepped inside. It was like coming home.

She closed her eyes and breathed in the smell of cardboard boxes and postage ink. She hung her purse on "her" hook before she slipped out of her sweater and dropped it on top. She had intentionally brought her fluffiest sweater. The one with huge pockets. Pockets that were big enough to slide a bag of drugs into and go unnoticed. She looked behind her. Except for the camera that was going to videotape everything.

She glanced up in time to see Detective McIntyre's car drive by. The plan was for her to park down at the end of main street in front of the hardware store. That way she could keep an eye on the computer monitor and get over there as soon as Tammy did her dirty deed!

Her eyes narrowed at the thought. She shook her head, determined to focus on something else.

The place was a bit of a mess. Things had been moved around. Ruth had everything meticulously organized at the post office and now nothing was in its place.

She opened the top drawer behind the customer counter. The one she used the most. Headlights flashed into the window as someone pulled down the alley. *That must be Tammy,* she thought.

She felt her cheeks warm and her blood begin to boil. *Get a grip, Ruth. Be cool*, she told herself. She took a deep breath and willed herself to remain calm when what she really wanted to do was attack Tammy and scratch her eyes out with her fingernails. The mental image made Ruth smile, just a tad.

Soon this will all be over and *she* will be the one in prison, Ruth reassured herself. She forced a smile to her face and spun around in time to see Tammy step through the rear door.

Ruth was convinced Tammy's smile was as fake as Ruth's own. "It's so good to see you, Ruth," she smiled brilliantly.

Ruth bared her teeth and smiled in return. "I'm glad to be back at work." That wasn't a lie. Ruth was thrilled to be back at the post office.

Tammy hung her sweater on the hook next to Ruth's. "I guess Kenny will be back in a few days." Ruth nodded, then turned back to the task at hand.

She prayed she would have the strength to keep her mouth shut. Ruth was grateful the post office opened right after Tammy showed up. The lobby filled up fast. The entire town of Belhaven had heard that Ruth was back and they stopped by to show their support.

Ruth teared up every time one of them told her how much they missed her. Even Gloria stopped by to check on Ruth. She leaned over the counter and gave Ruth a quick look. "How's it going?"

Ruth straightened her lips. "Okay. I'll be glad when this is over," she spat out through clenched teeth.

Gloria had an idea. How they could speed things up. Maybe give Tammy the perfect opportunity to plant the drugs. "How 'bout we run across the street to Dot's and grab a quick lunch."

Ruth started to shake her head until Gloria gave her a hard look. She slowly nodded when she realized what Gloria was doing. "Sure! Yeah! Great idea."

Ruth leaned around the corner. Tammy was shoving mail into the different slots. "Is it okay if Gloria and I run across the street and grab a quick bite?" Ruth's voice dripped with honey.

Tammy didn't look up. "Sure, yeah. It's slowed down a little so I should be able to handle it."

Ruth started for her purse, then stopped. She needed to leave it behind, to give Tammy a place to plant the drugs.

The girls wandered out the front door and headed for the street. When they were out of earshot, Gloria spoke words of encouragement to her friend. "You're doing great, Ruth. Just hang in there. It will be over soon enough."

Ruth nodded. "I just want to wrap my hands around her throat and throttle her!" she confessed.

Gloria touched her arm. "I know, I know. You don't want to go to prison for murder do you?"

Ruth grinned. She shrugged her shoulders. "But it might be worth it."

They slipped in the front door of the restaurant. Ruth picked a table by the window. She stared across the street at the post office, as if she had x-ray vision and could see Tammy's bad deeds through the brick exterior. "She's probably in there right now, sticking the stuff in my purse!" Ruth hissed under her breath.

Dot stopped by with a couple glasses of water. "Who's tending to the yard sale?"

Gloria looked up. "Jill and Lucy have it covered. First thing this morning we were busier than a one-armed wallpaper hanger." She twirled the straw in her glass of ice water. "It hit a lull so I thought I'd come into town to check on Ruth."

"Glad to see you back in the saddle, Ruth," Dot told her.

Ruth nodded. "Me, too. It's good to be back."

Ruth started to say, "I'll be glad..."

Gloria read her mind and cut her off. "...when the yard sale's over."

Ruth swallowed hard. She'd almost forgotten that only a few people knew about the sting.

Dot took their order and disappeared. "I almost slipped up," Ruth admitted.

"This has to say between the two of us," Gloria reminded her.

Dot stopped back a short time later with two turkey club sandwiches and a heaping mound of crispy French fries. Gloria was hungrier than she thought. Then she remembered Jill, Lucy and the boys still slogging it out at the yard sale. "Can I get two BLT's, two more turkey clubs and a bag of fries to go?"

"Sure can." Dot jotted down the order and disappeared again. By the time the to-go order was done, so was Ruth and Gloria. The post office was empty when they stepped back inside. Tammy was nowhere in sight. She must've heard the front door because she popped back in through the rear door looking a bit startled. "Oh, you ate fast."

Hopefully not so fast that you didn't have time to plant the drugs, Gloria thought to herself.

Tammy smiled brightly. "I'll step out for a bite now if you don't mind."

Ruth tried to smile back but she just couldn't pull it off, mainly because both she and Gloria knew that she was supposed to meet with Sharon on her lunch hour to let her know if Ruth had done anything "suspicious." If she had given Tammy any reason to believe Ruth should be searched before she left the post office.

Ruth's eyes shot daggers at Tammy's back when she left through the back screen door. She tapped her fingers on the gleaming countertop. "You think she did it?"

Gloria shrugged. "Yeah. I'd have to say she did." She was going to add that they'd know soon enough, but the post office door jingled and stopped Gloria from speaking.

Judith Arnett shuffled in through the front door. Gloria could see the poor woman was still in pain. She smiled when she saw Gloria. "Hi, Gloria. I'm surprised to see you here, what with the big sale going on at your place."

Gloria smacked the palm of her hand on her forehead. "Oh my gosh! I forgot about the sale!" She darted to the door, grabbed the handle then swung around. "Keep me posted on the other," she shouted out to Ruth before she ran to her car.

She got in, then remembered she'd left the lunches on the table at Dot's. She climbed back out of the car and took off across the street. Dot was waiting for her, the bag in hand. "I figured you'd be back!"

"Thanks, Dot!" She grabbed the bag and ran back out the door. She climbed back in Anabelle for the second time in as many minutes and started the car. She pulled out and onto the road just as Tammy and Detective McIntyre were pulling in.

She snapped her fingers. "Rats! I wish I could be here to see this!" But she had to run. She checked to make sure her cell phone was in her purse, certain that Ruth would call as soon as it was over and give her the blow-by-blow. Still, it wasn't as good as witnessing it in person!

The yard sale was back in action when Gloria pulled in. There had to be a dozen cars lined up beside the barn and down the road!

She grabbed the bag of food and made a beeline for the table where Lucy was sitting. She looked up from the table when she spotted Gloria. "I though you forgot all about us!"

"I'm sorry, Lucy! I got so caught up in Ruth's first day back at work, I forgot."

"How's it going?" Lucy was in on the sting. After all, she was the one that first caught

Tammy on camera slipping drugs into Ruth's purse.

Gloria rolled her eyes. "Whew! Ruth's fit to be tied." She chuckled. "Man, if looks could kill, Tammy would've died hours ago!"

Jill and the boys wandered over. Tyler opened the bag and looked inside. The boys had been hard at work in the garden all morning. Gloria was thankful for the help.

It seemed that every summer, the garden was a little bit harder to handle. Or maybe it was time for Gloria to think about slowing down and consider planting a more manageable garden. She did it partly for the fruits and vegetables she could use all winter, but there was another reason. She did it in honor of James. James loved the garden. When he was alive, their evening ritual was to wander through the garden and check on the plants. Keeping the garden alive was like keeping a small part of him alive.

Ryan pulled her from her thoughts. He grabbed a small handful of fries from the paper bag and stuffed them in his mouth. "Grams promised to teach me 'n Tyler how to drive the tractor."

Jill raised her eyebrows. "She did, did she?"

Gloria handed a BLT to Tyler and nodded over his head. "It's time. They're old enough now," she said.

She grabbed the other BLT and put it in Ryan's outstretched hand. "Your Father would be thrilled knowing the boys love the farm as much as they do."

Jill choked back sudden tears. It stung every time her Mom mentioned her Dad. Not just for herself, but for the years her two sons didn't have their grandfather in their life. It had only been a few years now, but the boys had been young when he died. Each year that passed, his memory would fade even more. "You're right,"

Gloria's daughter whispered. "Dad would love it."

"It looks like I missed lunch." A deep male voice drifted over Gloria's shoulder. A familiar voice. It was Paul! She spun around and faced him. He gave her a warm hug and kissed her cheek. "I had a call a couple miles up the road and thought I'd drop in to see how the sale was going." He looked at the groups of people sifting through the tables. "I should've brought some of my stuff over."

Gloria slapped his arm. She narrowed her eyes. "I told you!"

He lifted his hands in self-defense. "I know, I know," he admitted. He leaned in towards Gloria and whispered in her ear. "I heard your company moved out."

Ryan stepped between the two of them and pushed them apart. He eyed Paul suspiciously. "Grams is going to teach us how to drive the tractor," he told Paul.

Gloria couldn't get over how excited the boys were about driving the tractor. She made a mental note to spend some time thinking about what other stuff around the farm they might be interested in. She could see if the Palmers down the road would let her come by with the boys so they could feed the chickens and check for eggs...

Tyler puffed up his chest. "We helped Grams with the garden *and* cleaning the barn last night," he informed Paul.

Paul nodded somberly. "Your grandmother is lucky to have grandsons like you. I wish I had grandsons."

Ryan's eyebrows shot up. "You don't have any?" He thought every grandparent had grandsons. He wasn't so sure about girls...

Paul shook his head. "Nope. I have granddaughters but no grandsons."

Ryan slipped his hand into Gloria's. "Maybe Grams can bring us by to help you sometime," he offered. "Right, Grams?"

Gloria's heart melted right then and there! She had the most precious grandchildren on the planet!

"I would like that very much." Paul glanced at his watch. "I have to get back to the station." Gloria walked him to the car and watched as he climbed in. He pulled the door shut and rolled down the window. He nodded toward the boys, who were still eating their lunch. "You have some fine grandsons," he told her.

Gloria stiffened her back and smiled. "I couldn't agree more."

He started the car and put it in reverse. "I'll call you later tonight?"

She nodded, then leaned in the window and kissed his lips. "I'll be waiting," she flirted, then batted her eyes. The smile never left his face as he swung the car around and pulled onto the road.

Ryan finished his food and started to chase Mally around the yard. Tyler took his final bite of sandwich then wadded up the wrapper and tossed it in the empty bag. He had watched as Gloria told Paul good-bye. "Is that your boyfriend, Grams?"

Gloria studied the serious expression on his face. "Yes, Tyler. Paul is my boyfriend."

He nodded. "Are you going to marry him?"

The talk at the table stopped. Everyone turned to look at Gloria. Lucy. Jill. She stared at the road where his car had just been. "Maybe, Tyler. Maybe." That was the best answer she had to give.

Ruth was inside the post office, waiting on a customer when Tammy returned. She wandered in the back door and hung her jacket and purse next to Ruth's. The customer left. Ruth focused her attention to Tammy. "Did you have a nice lunch?"

"Yeah. Just had to run a few errands." She quickly turned her back to Ruth and began to sort through the packages that had accumulated throughout the morning.

Ruth turned back to the lobby when she heard the front door chime. It was Detective McIntyre. She walked to the counter. "How are you today, Ruth?"

Ruth smiled cautiously. "Great. Busy," she added.

While they made small talk, a plainclothes agent stepped in through the back door. The man made his way to the center of the room and nodded at Sharon. "Unfortunately, I'm here on official business," Sharon announced.

Ruth caught a glimpse of a sneer on Tammy's face when she heard the detective's words. Sharon stepped back over to the front door. She flipped the lock and switched the door sign to "Closed."

She stepped through the small half-door that separated the lobby from the employee area. She nodded to the detective, then pulled a computer from the bag that was slung over her shoulder. She set the laptop on the mail sorting counter in the rear. She looked at Ruth and then waved Tammy over.

The two women peered over Sharon McIntyre's shoulder and at the computer screen. The back of the post office came into view. Detective McIntyre pressed a few buttons. Tammy backed up a bit while Ruth moved closer. Close enough to have a clear look at the screen.

She motioned Tammy forward. "You need to see this."

Tammy swallowed hard and shuffled closer. The detective pressed one more button. Suddenly, there was an unobstructed view of Tammy. They all watched as she waited on a customer. Moments later, the customer exited the post office.

Tammy glanced around the room and out the window. She disappeared out the back screen door before returning seconds later. She was wearing latex gloves and had a small packet in her hand.

She glanced around the room before she walked over to Ruth's purse that was hanging on the hook. She opened the purse and dropped the small packet inside. She snapped the purse shut, peeled off the gloves and dropped them in a nearby trash can. For good measure, she reached down and sifted through the trash until the gloves disappeared from sight.

Detective McIntyre stopped the recording and turned to Tammy, whose face was pale as a ghost. "Go get Ruth's purse," she instructed in a quiet voice.

Tammy dropped her eyes and shuffled over to the bag. She lifted it off the hook and returned to where Ruth and the detectives were waiting. She set it on the counter next to the laptop.

The male detective nodded. "Open it."

Tammy wiped her brow with the back of her hand. "Do I have to?"

Sharon McIntyre nodded. "Yes."

Tammy reached down and unclasped the hook. She opened the purse then slid it towards Ruth. Ruth peeked in. The plastic bag they had all watched Tammy drop inside was still there, sitting on top.

Detective McIntyre grabbed a thin, plastic glove from her case and slipped it on before she reached in and pulled the small packet out. She turned to Ruth. "Is this yours?"

Ruth shook her head. "I've never seen that before in my life."

The detective turned to Tammy. "What's in the bag?"

"I-uh. I don't ..."

Sharon McIntyre cut her off. "You're under arrest for drug trafficking, drug possession, possession of an illegal substance."

The other detective took over. "You have the right to remain silent..."

"You can't arrest me!" Tammy turned on Ruth. "There's the criminal!" Tammy started to bawl.

Ruth almost felt sorry for her. Almost. She watched as Tammy was handcuffed then led out the back door to the unmarked police car.

Detective McIntyre turned to Ruth. "You know you're not supposed to have that in here." She pointed to the camera.

Ruth nodded. "I'll take it down," she promised.

"That's what I would advise. Of course, I can't force you to do anything." She winked at Ruth. "It saved your hide."

"No kidding!"

A light tap sounded on the front door. A customer's face was plastered to the outside of the glass entrance door. Two eyes peered in.

Ruth headed to the door. "I better open up."

Detective McIntyre nodded. She packed up her laptop and stuck it in her briefcase. She looked at the wastebasket. The one with Tammy's gloves inside. "I have to take that with me."

Ruth nodded. "Be my guest." As long as she wasn't going to arrest her, the woman could take whatever she wanted.

She unlocked the front door and let Bea in. Beatrice or "Bea" as she was called, stepped into the lobby. Bea was the local hairdresser and a noted gossip. "I'm so glad to see you're back." She'd been anxiously waiting for Ruth to return to work. "Say, did you hear that Sheriff Nelson is dating Sally Keane?"

Ruth shook her head. Right before she closed the door, she looked out at the bright blue sky, took a deep breath and smiled wide. All was right in Ruth's world once again. "You don't say?" She closed the door.

Chapter 10

Gloria watched as the last car pulled out of her drive. The yard sale was officially over. Her yard sale helpers had left a short time ago. Lucy and Jill offered to stay and help clean up but there was little left to take care of.   The place had been cleaned out. Things that Gloria thought would never sell were some of the first items to go.

She wandered into the barn and dropped the few remaining items into nearby boxes. She shoved them to the side and folded the legs on the gray card table.

Back inside the house, she slid the metal container across the table and pulled the stacks of bills from within. Between Ruth's investigation and the yard sale, she hadn't had time to figure out how much money they had made.

She sorted the piles - $20 bills, $10 bills, $5 bills. The largest of the stacks was the $1's. When she finished counting, she couldn't believe the amount. She grabbed her cell phone off the table to make a few phone calls with the good news when she noticed the text message. Her eyebrows furrowed. Why hadn't she noticed this earlier? Then she remembered. Judith Arnett had forwarded her a picture. The one she had snapped of Tammy and a shadowy figure out behind the post office the other night.

She slipped on her reading glasses and studied the picture up close. The investigators were convinced someone that worked at the post office was involved in the drug trafficking. *Was it Kenny?* She tapped the screen and zoomed in.

The figure's arm was lifted and at an angle as the person handed a box to Tammy. There, on the back of the arm, just above the elbow, was a design. Gloria walked over to the kitchen sink and flipped on the light. She held the phone directly under the light. The design was a tattoo – some kind of snake or dragon.

She clicked out of the picture and dialed Ruth's number. "How did it go?"

"Tammy confessed to everything after she saw that she was caught on camera planting the drugs in my purse," Ruth said. "Seems she was determined to get my job since Belhaven post office is bigger and nicer. Plus, the pay is better than at Fenway. That was her main motivation for framing me. Of course, she probably liked the money she was getting as the middle man in the drug ring, too."

"Detective McIntyre seems to think there's still another person involved," she added. "Someone that works at the Belhaven post office." She sighed. "I sure hope it's not Kenny."

Gloria nodded. "I hope not, either." She told Ruth how Judith had done a little surveillance work and managed to snap a picture of Tammy outside the post office handing a box to someone. "Does Kenny have a tattoo on the back of his arm?"

"Hmm. Well, I never noticed. It's possible."

"Any way to find out?" Gloria asked.

"Kenny's coming back to work in the morning," Ruth told her. "I'll check it out and get back to you."

There was another reason Gloria had called. "I just counted our money. We each made just over $500."

"Oh! Gosh, Gloria. That's great!" Ruth could use a little extra cash. She had her eye on a new surveillance camera. One that was more powerful and had a better microphone on it.

"I'll bring it by in the morning," Gloria told her.

After she hung up the phone, she decided against calling the rest of the girls. Instead, she'd surprise them tomorrow. Today had been a long day and she was exhausted. All she wanted to do was settle into her recliner with a frozen dinner and watch TV. Monday nights featured the "Monday Marathons" for her favorite TV series, "Detective on the Side."

She microwaved her meal, grabbed a jar of treats for Mally and Puddles and headed to the living room. The three of them settled into the recliner for a cozy evening at home.

Gloria and Mally were up bright and early the next morning. Gloria had a long to-do list that started with a visit to the post office. Gloria stepped through the front door. Ruth spied Gloria right away. She had that "I'm-about-to-explode" look on her face. She didn't wait for

Gloria to get to the counter. Instead, she met her at the door.

She grabbed her arm and pulled her to the corner. "Kenny's here but I can't see his arm! He has a long-sleeve jacket on!"

Gloria nodded. She had an idea. "Let me handle this."

Ruth headed back behind the counter and Gloria walked up to the customer side. She set her purse on the counter and opened it up. She plucked Ruth's share of the yard sale money from inside and pushed it across the counter. "Here's your share of the yard sale money," she said in a loud voice. "You'll never guess what I'm going to do with my share."

Ruth answered in the same loud voice. "What's that, Gloria?"

"I'm tossing around the idea of getting a tattoo! But I'm not sure how expensive they are."

Ruth's eyes widened. "Really?" she mouthed the words to Gloria.

Kenny dropped three boxes in one of the bins marked, "airport." He wandered over to the counter. "Hi Kenny." Gloria smiled.

"I heard you say you were gonna get a tattoo, Mrs. Rutherford," he said. "What kind?"

Gloria's face went blank. What kind of tattoo would she get? She hadn't the slightest idea... But the more she thought about it, the more she was intrigued by the idea. After all, none of her small circle of friends had one. She wondered if it hurt.

"I wonder how painful it is."

Kenny shook his head. "It's not too bad," he assured her. "Here, I'll show you what mine looks like."

Gloria's heart sank as she watched Kenny slip out of his jacket. She looked over at Ruth. The color had drained from her face.

Kenny set his jacket on the counter, then lifted his shirt to show his bare chest. "I got it a couple years back. On the front of Kenny's chest, just under his collarbone was an anchor with an eagle. In the middle was the earth. Above that were the words *Semper Fi*.

Gloria leaned in for a closer look. "That's a military tattoo."

Kenny nodded. "Marines."

Ruth snapped her fingers. "That's right. You were in the Marines."

Kenny nodded. "Yep. This is the only tattoo I'll ever have or ever want." He looked up. "Cool, huh?"

Gloria had to agree. It was cool. And Kenny was officially off the hook.

He pulled his shirt back down. "Now Seth's tattoo. His is one I don't really care for. Some kind of serpent with a satanic head on it."

Ruth spoke first. "I didn't know Seth had a tattoo."

"Yep." Kenny pointed to the back of his arm, above the elbow. "Right there. I asked him one time what that meant and he never did answer." He shrugged his shoulders. "Course, you never can tell about those college kids. The things they do after a night of drinking and partying."

Gloria nodded. They had their inside man. Seth Palmer. Part-time postal worker, full-time student....and drug dealer.

Ruth gave her a dark look. "I need to step outside for a second," she said to Kenny. She grabbed her cell phone and went out the back door.

Gloria glanced at her watch. "I better get going. I have more stops to make." She headed to the door. She opened it up and turned around. "It's nice to see you back at work, Kenny."

Kenny looked up from his mail sorting, a huge grin crossed his face. "I'm glad to be back, Mrs. Rutherford."

Gloria stopped by Dot's place where she ran into Lucy. She pulled out a chair and slumped down. She peered into Lucy's mug. "Is that coffee?"

Lucy shook her head. "Nope. I've switched over to hot chocolate."

Gloria rolled her eyes. "I have never seen anyone with a sweet tooth like yours."

Dot sidled over. She poured a coffee for Gloria. Gloria reached inside her purse and pulled out two wads of cash. Each wad had a rubber band around it. She handed one to Dot and set the other next to Lucy. "$547 each."

Lucy's eyes widened. "Wow! Each of us made that much?"

Gloria nodded. "That'll buy you a whole lot of hot chocolate," she teased.

Dot stuck her hand on her hip. "If I ate half the sweets Lucy ate, I'd weigh a ton!"

Lucy pushed the plate of sweet confectionary treats towards Gloria. "Here, have one."

"Thanks, but I think I'll pass this time," she said.

Dot nodded towards the post office across the street. "How's it going over there? I haven't noticed any unmarked cop cars so that's a good sign."

"I stopped by first thing this morning," Lucy chimed in. "Ruth is in high spirits."

"I predict the investigation will be wrapped up by the end of today," Gloria said.

Lucy leaned in. Dot leaned over.

Gloria leaned back. "What?"

"You know something," Lucy guessed.

Gloria lifted her coffee cup and peered over the rim. She shifted her eyes to the post office. They would all find out soon enough. She didn't want to steal Ruth's thunder. It would be up to her to share the story. She shook her head at her friends. "I better go. I have to stop by Margaret's place yet."

She drained the last few drops of coffee from the cup and pushed her chair back.

"What are you going to do with your little windfall?" Lucy asked.

Gloria shrugged her shoulders. "I was thinking about getting a tattoo."

She turned toward the door and missed the jaw drop on both her friends as they watched her walk out. Gloria grinned. She could never envision herself getting a tattoo, but it was fun to tease her friends.

Margaret wasn't home. Her husband, Don, answered Gloria's knock. Gloria handed him the envelope and told him it was the yard sale money. He took the envelope. "She should be back anytime."

Gloria shook her head. "I'd love to wait but I have one more stop to make," she explained. She waved good-bye, then headed to her car.

On the way to Andrea's place, Gloria cell phone rang. It was Ruth. "You'll never guess what!" she shouted.

"Seth confessed," Gloria guessed.

"Yep! Apparently, Tammy was trafficking the drugs through the Fenway post office. When she got wind the Feds were investigating, she talked Seth into helping her move them to the Belhaven post office."

Gloria nodded. That made sense.

Ruth went on. "Tammy would give Seth a heads-up when a package was coming. He would intercept it when it arrived at the post office, then hide it in the dumpster before he left that night. Tammy would come pick it up sometime during the night."

"Sounds like they had it all figured out," Gloria said.

"Yeah, that Tammy. Wow! She tried to frame me, get me out of the picture so she could continue on with her illegal trafficking PLUS take my job while she did it!"

Gloria shook her head. You never could tell about people, that's for sure!

She pulled into Andrea's and parked behind her car. "I gotta get going, Ruth. Call me later," she said.

She hung up the phone and slid out of the car. She hadn't seen her young friend for a couple days now. Between Ruth's crisis, the yard sale and last but not least, her grandsons visit, she'd been busy.

Gloria grinned when she looked at the lion's head knocker. For some reason, it cracked her up every time she saw it. Andrea opened the door, a frantic look on her face. "You got my message," she said.

"No. What message?" Gloria wondered.

"The one I left on your home phone," Andrea answered.

"I left the house first thing this morning and haven't been back," Gloria said.

Andrea waved Gloria inside. "You're never going to believe this," Andrea said. "My parents are coming for a visit."

She followed Andrea through the living room and library then out to the kitchen. "Well, that's great news! I can hardly wait to meet your parents."

Andrea whirled around, her eyes wide. "You don't understand. My parents are *different*."

They were in the kitchen now. Andrea pulled out a barstool and slumped down. She leaned her forehead in the palm of her hand. "What am I going to do?"

Gloria looked around. "Wait a minute. Something's different." She stared at the gleaming countertop. "The wall! You took out the wall!"

Andrea lifted her head. Her eyes lit up. "You like it?"

Gloria nodded her approval. "It sure did open up the space." She spun around. "Great job, Andrea. It turned out beautifully."

Andrea's expression turned glum again. "I planned to have a big get-together. You know, a housewarming party and invite everyone, but now I have my parents coming."

That didn't seem like much of a problem to Gloria. Her parents could help her out. They would have a chance to meet the people that were in their daughter's life. A chance to meet Brian.

Gloria patted her hand. "My dear. I can't wait to meet your parents. I can't wait for your party. It will all turn out. You'll see," she said.

But you don't know my parents, Andrea thought to herself.

The end.

Spaghetti Pie

<u>Ingredients</u>

6 ounce package of spaghetti, cooked and drained
2 Tbsp. butter or olive oil
1 large egg, beaten
1 cup grated Parmesan cheese
1 cup ricotta cheese
1 cup spaghetti sauce
¾ cup shredded mozzarella or Italian blend cheese

<u>Directions</u>

- Preheat oven to 350 degrees.
-Toss cooked and drained spaghetti with butter or olive oil.
- Mix 1/2 cup parmesan cheese with beaten egg. Stir into spaghetti.
-Pour spaghetti mixture into lightly greased 10" pie pan. (Glass baking dish works best for this recipe.)
-Press or mold spaghetti into a "crust."
-Spread ricotta cheese over top of spaghetti crust.
-Spread spaghetti sauce on top of ricotta cheese.
-Bake uncovered at 350 degrees for 25 minutes.
-Remove from oven. Top with mozzarella or Italian blend cheese.

-Return to oven and bake for another 5 minutes or until the cheese melts.

-Remove from oven. Sprinkle with remaining parmesan cheese.

-Cool for 10 minutes, then cut into wedges.

About The Author

Hope Callaghan is an author who loves to write Christian books, especially Christian Mystery and Cozy Mystery books. Born and raised in a small town in West Michigan, she now lives in Florida with her husband.

She is the proud mother of one daughter and a stepdaughter and stepson. When she's not doing the thing she loves best - writing books - she enjoys cooking, traveling and reading books.

Hope loves to connect with her readers!

Visit hopecallaghan.com for information on special offers and soon-to-be-released books!

Email: hope@hopecallaghan.com

Facebook page:
http://www.facebook.com/hopecallaghanauthor

Other Books by Author, Hope Callaghan:

DECEPTION CHRISTIAN MYSTERY SERIES:

Waves of Deception: Samantha Rite Series Book 1
Winds of Deception: Samantha Rite Series Book 2
Tides of Deception: Samantha Rite Series Book 3

GARDEN GIRLS CHRISTIAN COZY MYSTERIES SERIES:

41763205R00180

Made in the USA
Lexington, KY
26 May 2015